PLAYING THE HERO

The hero. The big-time gunman showing the roughs. Saving a halfwit girl . . . How Holliday would have laughed.

"God damn you," the red-headed man said. He looked mad as fire. "What have you done to Willy? You've cut him, damn you!" And he was on his feet and coming for Link on the jump.

Too many of them. Too many for even a "hero" to fist-fight. And god knew Link couldn't shoot them down, not for his own stupidity. And way too late to bow out gracefully. Christ, he'd sliced this poor fool in the blue checked shirt to a fare-thee-well. He'd have to push it through—and all his own damn fault!

The red-headed man came swinging—looked strong as a horse—Link ducked and dodged away, took a punch on his shoulder that knocked a grunt out of him, and came back with the toothpick. He swung the blade up the redhead's naked belly. The blade flashed in a gold ribbon of sunlight. The redhead put his hands down to stop it, and Link windmilled the knife down, away, and back up and around overhand, and struck the man in the forehead with the butt of the handle. It made a sharp, hard, whacking sound, and the red-headed man made an odd springing jump and fell over against the bales.

Link had learned long ago not to let men catch their breath in a fight. He jumped at the other two men. They stepped back. He drew the Bisley and cocked it.

Also in the BUCKSKIN Series:

BUCKSKIN #4

COLT CREEK

Roy LeBeau

LEISURE BOOKS ∞ **NEW YORK CITY**

A LEISURE BOOK

Published by

Dorchester Publishing Co., Inc.
6 East 39th Street
New York, NY 10016

Printed in the United States of America

BUCKSKIN #4

COLT CREEK

CHAPTER 1

LONG VALLEY lay cold, grey, black-branched, snow-streaked still in the early mountain Spring. The morning wind came booming down from the peaks, flowing through the great valley's length like a shifting insubstantial river of ice. The sunrise still struck across the mountainsides in rich reds and golds, barely breaking the last wide shadows of the night.

At the far end of the valley, a single speck appeared, moved very slowly deeper into the valley's mile-wide bowl, and more slowly still resolved itself into a single rider and his mount.

Link eased the brown along. The gelding was going lame, had been stumbling since they'd cleared the pass below Willow Falls—not that there'd been any waterfall there—or any willows, either. It had been a hard-rock mining town, nasty as one of the shovel fights the miners so enjoyed. Enjoyed watching, anyway.

Hard times had come down heavy on Willow Falls. No work there for a lean, starved-out drifter with a scarred cheek, cold grey eyes and grey in his hair as well, without nothing of value about him, except the fancy Bisley model Colt's strapped around the fringed waist of his long buckskin jacket, the soft hide greasy and blackened by the smoke of a wandering year's worth of campfires.

No work for a man like that—carried himself more like a sport, than a working man. Appeared to have some fancy airs about him, too, for a drifter too broke to buy a piece of pie. Seemed to be playing a hard-case, as well, the way he had of looking a man down who'd said hardly anything at all to him.

No work for a man like that. Sure as hell not in Willow Falls, where good miners went begging. If he was such a fancy-Dan, such a hard-case, then let him eat pride. Let him eat that and fill his belly with it. . .

Link pulled the brown up and swung off him, stiff in the morning cold. The horse was laming out . . . shouldn't be ridden at all now. Link led the horse on, walking as lightly as he could over the hard-frozen ground, trying to ease the jarring of his boots. The brown limped along behind, head down, tuckered out and bone weary.

Link had bought him from a banker in Laredo, a fair enough deal. The brown had not been much horse at the time, just worth his price. He was less horse now. Link felt no fondness for him. He'd never liked cold-blooded horses, and the brown was thick to the bone. A heavy, slow horse, stupid and stubborn.

Link felt the sun's first heat on the back of his neck as he walked, and the morning's hunger-pains with it. Two days since he'd eaten. Two days and a bit, come to think of it. He'd shot a rabbit back then. And more to consider than that. He'd lost, gambling.

Not just in one game—nothing to be concerned about there. He lost in every game, in Willow Falls and before Willow Falls, a terrible bad streak. Every penny he owned, and his saddle-bags thrown in.

8

There was a day he hadn't lost like that when he played. Was a day he'd not played at all for fear it would lead to trouble of some kind—that he'd have to draw and shoot out of . . . He'd been mighty nice in those days, mighty nice about what he did.

Now, he'd run out of nice. Out of a clean shirt. Out of his money. Out of a decent horse. Out of being young, too. That was something he'd run out of awhile back. He'd damned near run out of his name, too. Didn't hear much about Buckskin Frank Leslie these days. Sometimes just talk . . . the old, sad story . . . the girl . . . the Thompsons. Holiday.

Didn't hear much about that, these days. Come a day he could use his name, and nobody would give a damn.

Charmain Swazie had been an hour trying to get the Sheriff out of bed. It was not a problem of liquor and overindulgence, although in his youth Swazie had overindulged with the best. It was age, now. And rheumatism.

Swazie, in his youth, had been a formidable fellow: short, fierce, thick-set and strong as a young ox. A lawman born. Years and years ago, all that was. Towns and towns ago, too. More towns than Charmian Swazie cared to count, late-married though they were, or to remember. Not that Charley Swazie had ever been a famous badge-man. He had never been that—more prone to use his fists on a bad man than to call him out and kill him in the street. For that reason, he'd been called "Copper" Swazie, sometimes, by his companion deputies—more of a policeman than a frontier lawman, they felt. Swazie should have been on some city force, perhaps, in a blue-uniform job he might have retired from with honor. And, Charmian felt with a passion, some decent pension for all the dangerous duties he had performed so steadily.

It was so unfair that Charley Swazie, the strength of his youth long gone, should still have to strive to keep peace in such a vicious little town as Colt Creek. It was unfair, and it was dangerous. Charley Swazie was sixty-four years old. And tired. In the last few years, the high-mountain winters had bent him down, and swollen the joints of his arms and legs so that it took a good hour to get the poor little man up and out of bed. And he talking away, and joking all the while, and trying to stretch out his arms and exercise them. Charmian knew how it hurt him, and it broke her heart every morning.

Someday soon, when they tired of playing with him, the Coes would kill Charley Swazie.

"Old girl, dammit! That's enough! You put any more of that damned concoction on me and I'll stink up the town!" Charmian had been rubbing his back with a sovereign grease of duck-fat, assefoedita, rue, and Pettis's Ointment.

"Oh, shut up," Charmian said to the sheriff.

Link saw the town from a little rise about a half-mile out. It wasn't much to see. A long curving main street, lined with peeled-log buildings on each side for a hundred yards or so, with a few short side streets— alleys would be a better name for them—crossing it at intervals. Buggies, wagons, and a scattering of saddle mounts were slowly churning up the icy mud, pasing back and forth on their owners' errands. Link had seen a hundred—a thousand—towns just like it.

A strong smell of mingled wood-smoke and horse-manure came blowing over the rise. Link had smelled a thousand towns like that, too; and after weeks on a hungry trail, it smelled damned good. His feet were frozen wood within his boots, his hand cramped and frost-stiff on the lame brown's reins. A poor morning for a walk. A pretty day, clear as hotel crystal, but too damn cold for a man afoot in a thin buckskin jacket. And he despised going into a new town walking, leading a lame horse down Main Street. That sort of entrance marked a man in a cow-town.

Link looked back at the brown. The horse was holding his sore foot up off the ground. Link sighed; he wasn't quite low enough yet to ride a hurting horse just for show. He'd skirt Main Street, down there, walk down and around and come up one of the side streets as if he'd just dismounted for the town traffic. It would mean an extra quarter-mile walking, for sure.

He said, "God damn it to hell," and stepped out, wincing as his boots thudded on the frozen mud. The brown farted, and came hobbling after him, shaking its head so its bit-chain jingled. Both their breaths puffed frosty in the icy air.

Perry Patterson had bought the livery stable from an Irishman named Cleary just before the War Between the States. (Patterson called it that, although most men in town called it the Civil War.) Patterson, who had been born in Alabama and fought with the Alabamas in the Wilderness before coming back West to Colt Creek, still harbored a fine hatred of Yankees and of Westerners who had fought with them. He was not a trouble-maker, but he kept men marked in his mind, depending on which side they'd fought on.

He opined, at first, that this Mr. Fred Link had been a Reb. That, because of his apparent poverty, Patterson having observed that Yankees and those who fought with them seemed to have a neater eye for a dollar than old Confederates did. And even with the war years over, there by God were still advantages in having been a Blue-belly! Government contracts, for

11

one. The cavalry, now, over in Fort Snell, would sooner bust a gut than give their town-stalling business to B-Street Livery-Rental-and Board. A half-drunk halfbreed like Marcy got every damn bit of government horse-business there was in the whole damn town. The cowboys didn't care either. They'd keep those poor animals of theirs standing out in the cold and rain till their hooves froze! It was a damned poor town for an honest man's business, and that was that.

This man, now, was sure to be meager business—if any business. Come walking up the street leading a lame horse . . . a piss-poor horse apparently, even in its best days. Nor was the leader any feast for a businessman's eye. Lean man . . . looked like a hungry man, in fact. Trail-worn and dead broke, if Perry Patterson was any judge, which he was.

Fellow wanted stalling for his plug—didn't ask the price, Patterson noticed—and something kept him from boning the man from the two bits in advance. Fellow had a damn cold eye . . . cold as winter. And, Patterson thought, probably had fought on the right side. He had a Confederate look to him.

Patterson called for Jean to take the horse. Man didn't say anything about fomentations and such; Patterson assumed he meant to treat the horse's leg himself. Every damn drifter thought he was the world's gift to horse-doctoring. Well, there you were . . . a man fought in the Wilderness and on the Just Side, by God. And what reward might you expect? Why, a failed stable in a murderer's town, with a cold-eyed walking tramp for your day's prime customer. That's what you might expect. That, and a half-wit niece, more boy than girl to look at and no better than a spotted dog-bitch in her behavior. Which hadn't been cured by any beating he'd been able to catch her for, the filthy, disgusting thing. More of an animal, when you came right down to it, than a decent human woman.

Link stood in the stableyard watching the bean-pole who seemed to own it slowly stilt up the steps to the stable office. An odd, slow-moving man, looked to have a sharp eye on Link's poor clothes and sad horse. Worried about his two bits more than likely. Then, a girl odder than the fellow came up to take the brown. Link thought she was a man at first, a stable boy, thought that "Jean" had been "Gene." But she was a girl, right enough, though not much for pretty. She nodded to Link, took the reins, and led the brown away into the stable, glancing down at the lame leg as she did. She was thin, with a long face and big jaw—looked a bit like a horse, herself. Washed-out eyes, a blank sort of blue, and no figure to speak of.

She pulled the horse up at the stable door, and called back to Link over her shoulder. She had a garbled way of speaking; it took Link a moment to realize she'd asked if she should doctor the horse's leg.

He'd known short-witted people before; oftener than not they had a way with animals. "Go on," he said, and nodded to her. "Doctor it up for me." She looked at him for a moment, then led the horse on into the stable, into the shadows there. Pants on her like a boy. Walked like one, too.

Link shouldered his war-bag—empty as a banker's smile—balanced the Henry in one hand, and walked out of the stableyard into the street. He grudged even the Henry's light weight. Grudged it as much because he'd never liked rifles very much for fighting, as for its light-hitting little cartridges. He'd had a buffalo gun, once. That had, at least, been an honest rifle. If you wanted to stand off a hundred yards or two and kill a beast or a man, a Sharps would do it, and no doubt about it, if that was your notion of sport, or a fight.

13

He walked on up the street—"B Street," a sign said —toward Main. That would be Main Street, for sure; cow-towns didn't waste much imagination on street-naming. There was plenty of traffic: goods wagons drawing slowly through the mud, and buckboards freighting supplies out to the ranches in the hills. There was action here, at least. It wasn't the dead town that Williow Falls had been. Kids in the street, too, and some ladies—at least they looked like ladies; it was hard to tell in cold weather, with the females and bundled up. He remembered the goose-pimples on the stable girl's skinny arms. It was a hard life, if you weakened. Hell, it was a hard life if you didn't.

Main Street—and it *was* Main Street—was even busier. More ladies, lots of dogs playing in the mud. People stomping along the rough-planked raised sidewalks, trying to keep their toes from freezing in their boots. He wriggled his own in the worn Mexican high heels. No feeling at all. It was time, and past time, to get his butt indoors and beside a stove.

Across the street and way down, Link saw a big, likely-looking saloon front. "The White Rose," the sign said. Two-storey frame with a fine carved false front for a third. Seemed to be having custom enough, drovers mostly, it appeared. Link had just seventeen cents on him. Enough for a nickel beer and a bite of free lunch with it. Time enough then, when his bones had thawed, to see about some work. Fence-fixing for one of the ranches, maybe, or some laboring job in town. Enough for a gaming stake. That was all he wanted. It was true there had been a time when he wouldn't gamble at all, not turn a single card for fear of a disagreement, an argument that might lead to a fight. A shooting.

Well, he'd still prefer that wouldn't happen. Sure as hell didn't need the questions—maybe the memories of some wide-traveled drummer who might remember Frank Leslie of Dodge City, and his wicked, fast gun. He didn't need it, that recognition, the way some old pistoleros seemed to, and didn't want it. But a man had to eat. Had to do more than that if he was a man. Should have a decent horse under him, and clean clothes on his back and at least the price of a bed and breakfast in his pocket. Not too much to ask, Link thought. Not all that damn much to ask. So, to hell with memories of what was and to hell with might have been, as well. He'd work for some money, and then he'd gamble with that. And he'd mind his own business while he did it. And should a man seek trouble with him? Well, that man would have to seek mighty hard to find trouble with Fred Link.

Mr. Link was a peaceable man.

He shouldered the war-bag, fended off a horseman splashing his way past the sidewalk, and plunged into the street, holding up halfway across to let a buckboard lurch past him, wheels caked with black mud.

The White Rose was as fancy inside as out. A sport-hall for sure, empty this early in the morning, or almost empty. Three men stood spaced along the bar, keeping a before-breakfast distance between them. Off to the other side of the wide room, a black swamper rattled among the tables stacked with upturned chairs. There was a job already spoken for. A man was working behind the bar, dressy in a black wool suit and derby hat. He was mopping the duckboard back there; Link knew from the motion of his back, the quick poke of mop-handle in the long mirror. The mirror could have used a mopping, too.

Link went up to the bar and asked the man behind it for a beer. The fellow turned, gripping his mop, and gave Link a good look at his gold studs. The owner, then, and impatient of bar-work, more than likely.

The derby sighed, went down the bar, drew a careless beer, and slid it back up to Link, too fast. Then he bent his head and went back to his mopping. Link put his nickel down loud enough for the man to hear it clink on the mahogany, and then looked around for the lunch counter. It was laid out toward the back of the room, past the end of the bar. He strolled over.

Not much left of last night's doings. A bowl of hard-boiled eggs, some slices off a stale rye loaf, a jar of pig's feet that looked considerable less than fresh, and a tangle of sliced onion on a big cracked dish. No cheese. No other meat. Still, Link did his best to make do. He palmed two of the eggs, selected, with some care, the two largest of the bread slices, and built himself a sizeable onion sandwich. He wished for mustard, but there was none—no pickles, either.

He balanced his fixin's in his right hand, picked out a pig's foot with his left, and steered toward a table the swamper seemed to have brushed off. He caught a glimpse of the gold studs out of the corner of his eye as he went. The fellow was watching him in the mirror, giving the glim to the onion sandwich, the two eggs and the pig's foot. For the White Rose, it was apparently a heavy breakfast to free-load off a nickel beer.

It meant the White Rose was bad run. Any canny saloon man knew to lay out a good free lunch, and heavy on the salt meats, too. You got it back at the bar and tables ten times over. Link had known of saloons and gambling dens where a damn good breakfast was served to late customers, and for nothing, or next to nothing. It led men to stay late, drinking and playing. More than worth the cost.

Gold-studs didn't know his business, this *was* his business.

The swamper hadn't done the table after all. Link

sat down facing the cleanest part, laid out his food, and then decided to try the pig's foot first. It was not likely to be the best of the meal.

It wasn't.

While he was chewing at it, the spit flooding into his mouth nevertheless, he heard one of the men at the bar say something to the Gold-studs, and chuckle. They were talking about him. He knew it, as he knew whenever he was the object of stranger's attention. It was an old gift, if you could call it that. A necessary gift, it had been.

Two of the three men at the bar were armed. Gold-studs was armed, too, with a Derringer, or some such little pistol, tucked under the side of his waistcoat. The swamper had no weapon on him.

Link could see the men at the bar from where he sat, and the owner, too. He could hear the black swamper messing with his broom behind him. He ignored the chuckle, finished the pig's foot, and began to eat his onion sandwich. It tasted wonderful, and he tried to chew as slowly as possible, to make it last. His jaws ached with the pleasure of the food, and it was a considerable source of satisfaction that he had his two hard-boiled eggs yet to eat.

The men at the bar were talking, but they weren't talking about him anymore.

When, some minutes later, Link swallowed the last of his food—the eggs *had* been the best of it—he got up and went back to the bar. Gold-studs and the man he'd been talking to turned to watch him as he came up to them.

"Sorry to interrupt your talk, gents," Link said. "But would you be the owner of this place?" to Gold-studs. Gold-studs surprised him by holding out a friendly enough hand, and nodding. "I would be, and I am," he said. He had a Scotch accent, just a slight

17

one. Born over there. "Name's MacDuff, like in the play." He was a stocky man, looked strong, and supported a very fine handlebar mustache. His eyes were brown and bloodshot.

"My name's Link." The other man smiled in a friendly way, and held out a long-fingered, pale hand. "Wilson Coe," he said. Link shook with him, and that hand was as soft and smooth as a little girl's. A smart-man's hand, that meant. Someone who did no droving, or mining, or farming for his living.

"Well, Mr. MacDuff," Link said, "I was curious if you might have a job opening for a bartender here."

"Looking for more free lunch," the soft-handed man said. Wilson Coe. It was an unpleasant thing to say, but he smiled at Link in the friendliest way, and winked at him as if they were friends. Link didn't smile back.

"Damn right I have an *opening*," MacDuff said. "Question is, can you fill it?" He gestured down the bar. "This is not just a mop-up job, Mister. It's a hard-serve job and then some! I have times at night I have maybe two hundred men ordering their pleasure from this bar here. You see, that takes a fella that knows his business."

"I know that business," Link said. "I've bartended in San Francisco, and in . . . Denver." He'd almost said, "Dodge City."

"San Francisco?" said Mr. Coe, raising his eyebrows. He smiled at Link and winked at him again. "We've got a big-town sport with us this morning, Ed!"

Link ignored him. "Try me," he said to MacDuff. MacDuff frowned, thinking it over. And if he thought he'd just as soon not, Link would be on his way, likely walking, to the stockyards east of town, to beg a job shoveling cowshit out of icy mud for ten cents a day.

He hadn't intended to say anything more but he did.

"Give me a try." It cost him a good deal to say that, to repeat himself that way.

But MacDuff gave him a hard look—took in the pistol, the worn, trail-dirty clothes, the scar across his cheek—and shook his head, *no*.

CHAPTER 2

"OH, NOW, why not let the fellow show his stuff?" Wilson Coe smiled at Link. "I'll bet this fellow can whip us up a fancy San Francisco cocktail in nothing flat!"

MacDuff glanced at Link, and shook his head. "Sorry, Mister, I can't—" But Coe interrupted him. "Sure you can, Ed." Coe wasn't smiling as much as he had. "Give this gentleman a chance, now, to show us what he can do. We'll call it a breakfast special."

MacDuff had gone some red in the face, but he glanced at Link again, and this time nodded. "All right. If you can come back here and make a mixed drink worth swallowing . . ." "A martini cocktail," Wilson Coe said. "Mix us one of those, the way the Palmer House serves them, in Chicago."

Link had seen that McDuff was getting bullied and was curious why he took it; money, or the lack of it, likely. Coe had the look of a banker about him. But if the bullying worked to Link's advantage, so much the better.

"I'll do it," he said, and stepped around the end of the bar. He walked down the duckboards—MacDuff had used too much water in his mopping—and bent to look into the cabinets under the liquor shelf. Dirty glasses and old bar-rags in the first two. Then he found one shelf of wine, and, in the back of a second shelf, dusty half-bottle of vermouth among whiskey jugs and chipped toddy glasses and straw-covered bottles of Italian wine no better than it should be.

The gin stood in the long line of bottles under the mirror and the ice-box was full of cracked chunks floating in dark water. Link rinsed a copper mixer at the sink and began measuring out two martinis. After ten years—more than ten years—it came back to him fresh as paint. Bartending.

How Holiday would have laughed to see him back at it. Buckskin Frank Leslie, gambler, pimp, gunman extraordinaire. Now, a little down on his luck, gone back to bartending, by God, to get himself a stake! Getting poker stake money had never been a problem for Doc. He'd yank out some bully's bad tooth, or borrow from a whore, or rob a stage, if he had to. Well, bartending was as honorable a profession as dentistry, and damned if Link wouldn't make a go of it. One week, maybe two weeks mixing drinks and paddling beer for a crowd of drunken drovers. Then, with maybe thirty or forty dollars wage and tip money, some slow, small-time little games, and build from there to a real stake, and better luck than he'd had lately to build it further.

He set two iced glasses up on the bar, shook the mixer with an easy circular motion, opened it, and poured the cocktails out. Give these damned rubes a taste of civilization . . .

MacDuff picked his drink up, snorted a mouthful down, and paused, licking his moustache. Wilson Coe took a careful sip of his, and his eyebrows went up. "My, my," he said. "It appears we have an artist among us." He smiled and winked at Link as if they were chums from way back.

MacDuff finished his drink, wiped his moustache with the back of his hand, and set the glass back onto the bar with a click. "Alright. You got a job—uh, what the hell was your name?"

"Link."

"All right. If you can handle a crowd. I'll pay twenty bucks a week, and that's damn good money! That's *if* you can handle a crowd. You won't see many of these cowpushers askin' you for a martini cocktail!"

Link nodded. He was ashamed of how grateful he felt, grateful even to the soft-handed dude who'd had his fun about it. Twenty dollars and what he'd kite off the cash-drawer would set him a poker stake in a couple of weeks, maybe three.

"My, my . . . MacDuff has achieved a new mixologist." Wilson Coe raised his glass to Link and the saloon-keeper. MacDuff went a little redder in the face, but didn't say anything, and Link noticed something odd. The two other men down the bar—they'd been there all along, nursing morning beers—had stayed where they were. No strolling down to join in the conversation, no asking for a sample of the new barman's goods for themselves. No friendly talk like that at all. They'd stayed put and minded their own business. Were still doing it.

Not angry; not hostile. Afraid.

But scared of who? Not red-faced MacDuff. And they didn't know Link from Adam.

Wilson Coe smiled at Link, winked as if they were old friends, and finished his martini. "The best breakfast beverage," he said, "and much appreciated." He slapped MacDuff on the shoulder. "See you in my office this afternoon, Ed. Don't be late." He turned from the bar, and walked out of the White Rose with a little backward wave of his hand by way of farewell.

The other two men at the bar watched him in the long bar mirror as he went.

"Now, you listen to me, Link," MacDuff said. He was still watching the door where Coe had gone out. "You got yourself hired, and that's all right. But you see you do the damn work, and don't you take one damn penny from that drawer! You do, and I'll fire your ragged butt right out of here, Wilse Coe, or no Wilse Coe!" He shouted across the room at the swamper. "George! Get your black ass back to the kitchen and rustle me my damn breakfast!" And to Link, "You remember what I said. I mean it, now!"

An hour later, full of a hot, greasy breakfast cooked for him by a silent George after MacDuff had finished his, Link sat on a narrow cot in the big liquor closet behind the bar, and warmed his hands at a dented little sheep-herder's stove. It was going to be home, and it felt like home, beer-stink and all. It was warm.

Boots still on, Link lay back on the cot's stained canvas cover. Belly full, and bones warm. For right now, it was enough. He felt himself starting to drift into sleep.

Sleep . . . sleep. A light sleep, skipping and restless. Odd dreams. Dreams better not dreamt—of a tall Appaloosa stud . . . and a mountain ranch . . . a girl. A big Irishman in a plug hat. Shooting . . . *shooting!* Link woke with a grunt, his hand already down on the Bisley's grip.

He heard another flat, cracking sound. Someone dumping a loud of lumber in the side street along the saloon's thin plank wall.

Link sighed, settling back onto the cot. No need to be so nervy. Nobody around here had any call to come shooting at a barkeep named Fred Link. No need for any trouble at all.

He lay still, listening to the muffled noises of the street outside, the faint scrape and rattle out beyond the bar as the swamper moved the chairs and tables into line. Must have finished mopping. Now, what were the chances of getting back to sleep? God knows he was tired enough. Used to be able to take a trail ride through three territories—chasing, or being chased, more often than not—and come out of that ride as fresh as a mountain flower. Not smelling as fine, maybe, but still mighty fresh. Past days. Long past, now . . .

He lay still for a while longer, comfortable in the heat of the little stove, trying to sleep. Then, after a while, he stopped trying, heaved himself up to sit on the edge of the cot, dug in his war-bag for oil and rags, and drew the Bisley and laid it on his lap to clean. He pulled the cylinder, unscrewed the handgrips, and levered out the hammer-spring as neatly as a gunsmith might have. Then he commenced to clean the piece, humming a little under his breath while he did it. Thinking about something else.

When the revolver was spotless and oil-filmed, he re-assembled it, wiped the five loads lightly with the oily rag, and slipped the rounds into the cylinder again, lowering the hammer on the empty. The holster could have used saddle soap . . . he'd have to ask a bit from the stable. Saddle could use it as well, of course.

And his clothes could use soaping. So could he. Must smell more than a little ripe. He'd have to get them to put a couple of kettles on for him in the kitchen, get the trail-stink scrubbed off. Do his clothes, too. They'd dry fast enough over that big stove back there.

He slid the Colt's back into the holster, stood up stiffly, stretched those kinks out as well as he could, buckled the revolver belt back on, and dug into the war-bag for the rest of his things. Not much there. A striped shirt with a torn sleeve, two cheap paper collars, a pair of wool trousers with a hole in the left knee, and a pair each of extra long-johns and socks. All dirty as Sadie's garter, all worn down and worn out.

He tucked the bundle under his arm, unlatched the liquor closet's narrow door, and walked through it and out behind the bar. The big room was empty, coldly lit only by the bleak northern light filtering through dusty windows. There'd be some people coming in in an hour or so for nooners. No one, now.

Two big pot-belly stoves glowed dull red, spaced across the room from side to side. Kept the place warm enough, anyway.

Link walked down the room, through a pair of stain-spotted red velvet curtains, and down the long, dark side passage to the kitchen. There were two fat girls sitting in the place when he walked in. Whores from upstairs. They were white girls, fat and puffy as biscuit dough, with hard black raisins for eyes. They looked like sisters.

An old Chinaman was standing behind the big kitchen range. He gave Link a sharp look when he came in, then gave him another. "Hello," he said. 'You the new bartender?" He didn't have a Chinky accent in his speech at all. He sounded like somebody from a city.

"I am."

The old man nodded. He had a round, wrinkled face, and hooded eyes. Just one or two teeth left in his bottom jaw, and a long, dirty-white beard that he wore tied doubled up with a knot of string—to keep it out of the soup when he cooked, Link figured.

The fat girls gave Link a nod when he went by the table. They were sisters for sure, and a poor sign of the quality of the White Rose if they were a sample of the best the place could offer.

"Mary and Mercy Kasmeir," the old Chinaman said, indicating the girls. "Deef 'n dumb" he added, lifting the cover of a pot. Smelled like a game stew of some kind. "Dummies."

"That's a good-smelling stew," Link said, figuring to butter up the old man for his laundry water. "Venison," the old man said, "for a private party tonight." He dropped the cover back on. "You want cleaning water off this stove?"

"I'd appreciate it."

The old man grunted, and lifted the lid of another pot. Beans. "This one for you people," and he grinned, showing his teeth. He had three in his lower jaw, four upstairs. "I can heat you that water. You get the black man to bring it in from the back." He stirred the beans.

Link dumped his clothes on the floor, and went out back, and down a shaky flight of steps to the muddy yard. The mud was half ice, half melt-water. The black man was chopping kindling by a lean-to wood shed.

"Boy," Link said, "I need some water for washing in there." The swamper stopped chopping, and stared at Link; he was a small, bony man, his eyes red and inflamed, the skin of his hands cracked and chapped raw pink in the cold. He didn't seem eager to do the work.

"I'd be obliged," Link said. And stood in the mud and stared at the man.

The swamper lowered his eyes and nodded, and Link turned and went back inside. It was a dank, raw day, as cold as the inside of an ice-box. He noticed the back steps as he went up them to the door. Rotted and falling apart . . . something to keep in mind, just in case it might be necessary to come running down those steps very fast some dark night. Link had long ago learned to check up on the back way out. "The back door is the best door," Masterson had said once at a dancing party in Fort Smith. And gone on to tell of a shooting scrape in Kansas, that he plain ducked out on. Two ace-slippers on the prod, with shotguns, had thundered in the front of a whorehouse on Academy street. Masterson had gone running out the back, fell off a porch he hadn't known was there, and lit square onto a pit-fighting dog the house pimp kept for betting on. All this in pitch dark.

The upshot had the dog lighting into Masterson in a serious way, while the two gamblers stood on the porch, shotguns cradled, laughing fit to pop. It had been a lesson to Masterson about investigating exits. Link had already learned his own lessons about that. Not as funny as Masterson's.

Odd about that man; many disliked him. Too humorous for their tastes, Link supposed. Nothing the matter with his guts, though, and a fine standing pistol shot, too, though not much for quick.

He walked back into the warm kitchen, and sat down with the girls at the big, scarred table. One of them made an odd sound in her throat, and nodded and smiled at him. Link nodded and smiled back. He assumed the noise was her way of talking. They were poor quality girls, right enough, for a busy little cow-town like this. For a big, handsome saloon like this, too. Now, the other girl—Link couldn't remember which one was Mary and which one was Mercy— made the same kind of noise and bobbed her head at him like a feeding hen. He smiled and bobbed his head back. He felt sorry for them, fat and ugly like they were. And whores, too. And deaf and dumb. It seemed a lot of punishment for two simple fat girls off a forty-acre claim somewhere.

A heave and clank at the back door, and the

swamper, George, came humping in two big buckets of well water; he set them down on the back of the stove, while the old Chinaman watched to see he didn't bump his cooking pots.

Link remembered the negro had cooked his breakfast for him, after all. "You got more buckets out there, George?" Link said. The swamper nodded, looking some sullen. Link got up from the table. "I'll need a couple more. Come on. I'll give you a hand." The negro brightened up, but not too much. It wasn't George's weather out there, and that was that.

It took Link more than an hour to scrub himself down standing behind the stove in the biggest of the buckets, and to soap, scrub, and wring out his clothes as well, and hang them on a frayed cord stretched over the length of the stove. The girls had paid no attention to his nakedness, just sat at the big table drinking coffee for a while, then moaned something to the old Chinaman, gotten up, and drifted out of the kitchen like two fat heifers changing pasture.

George had carried some kindling in for the pot-bellies, and then disappeared up the back stairs with a plate of beans for his lunch.

Link's clothes steamed dry quickly over the big cookstove. Thirty minutes after he'd hung them up, he was able to get into a pair of long-johns, a shirt, and a pair of slightly damp trousers, the wool ones, with the tear at the knee. Clean clothes, a full belly—two plates of the Chinaman's beans—and he was ready to help bartend the lunch-crowd out front.

The customers were already piling up, and MacDuffy's day-man was having trouble handling it. Link pushed through the crowd around the free lunch which still looked mighty thin pickings, even though there was more of it, now, and some sliced meat, too, and slid in behind the bar. The day-man glanced at him, at the revolver on his hip.

"Heard of you," he said, above the noise of the men shouting for their beers and whiskey shots. He was a tall man, young, not much more than a boy, with a glance that shied away when Link looked straight at him. He had an indoor look to him, and his teeth were stained brown with cheap snuff. "I'm Ross Parker—" He reached up to the long mirror shelf for a bottle of Pennsylvania whiskey "—and I'm sure glad to see you!" He looked toward the wide steps leading up from the faro tables to the narrow balcony that ran around the saloon's second floor. "Mr. MacDuff's all right, but he isn't too good back here." He poured the whiskey, and stepped to the tab to draw beers for two kid drovers. "We had another man, Hank Throckmorton. He was all right, but he quit—and I've got my Mom to look out for . . ." Link moved down the bar and started drawing beers beside him—draw, paddle off the foam, and pass the mug on down with an easy sweep of his hand, skating them down the mahogany and catching the nickels and occasional two-bit piece sliding back. His mind noting the calls without trying, lining the orders up and checking them off as he served. It was as automatic as one of those steam-drillers they used in foundries; feed a punched-out copper belt into the words and that was the pattern the machine drilled, every time.

It was enjoyable. It came back to him, more and more with every order. He'd glance up into the noisy crowd along the bar, mark his customers, note their pleasure, and serve it up. A couple of voices called for mixed drinks, a whiskey flip and a mulled wine cocktail. Link nodded the beer drinkers off onto Parker, turned a deaf ear to them, and mixed the flip, served it, heated the cup of wine over the spirit-lamp, splashed in brandy, found a nutmeg in the goods drawer, grated a half pinch into the wine, poured it steaming into a short glass, and slid it ten feet down the bar to stop just in front of the customer's watch-chain. Some men at the bar whistled and clapped, and Link caught the cash coming back up, palmed two bits, and dropped the nickels into the money drawer with a neat considerable jingle, aided by a flick of his finger in there as he did.

It was all coming back to him—the smooth, convivial pleasure of a warm, noisy crowd of drinkers, laughing, telling stories, joshing their friends, arguing, in friendly enough fashion around mouthfuls of ham sandwich.

Worse ways to make a living than tending a bar.

"My name's Link," he said to Parker when they crossed steps to pour rye shots for some drummers at the center of the bar. "Yeah, Mr. MacDuff told me," the boy said. After that, he tried twice to come up to Link's end of the bar to draw beer and Link had to gesture him back down the duckboards. Parker didn't even know enough to territory a service bar.

Link was paddling a three-mug handful of beer—it looked to be good quality brew, for local cooked; damn sure MacDuff didn't freight his draft up from Boise—when he looked up over the customers and saw MacDuff standing on the second floor balcony watching the action. No gambling action to watch that Link could see. MacDuff was checking the bar. Seemed pleased enough with what he was seeing. Link served the beers one right across, one further up, and the last sliding all the way down past Parker. Stopped dead in front of the customer's shirt-buttons. He collected the cash as it came, palmed forty cents right out of it, and jingled the rest into the money drawer.

He checked MacDuff's reflection off a facet on a

tumbler's base, an old bar-man's trick, and saw that the owner hadn't made the palm. Seemed real happy up there. Nothing better than a boss who stood shy of his cash drawer. Friendly way to be. At this rate, it wouldn't be three weeks to a stake. Two weeks would do it, and to spare.

Low thing to do, of course, petty thieving. There had been a time he'd have killed a man quicker than steal a biscuit. Old days—old ways. This was now, with now's necessaries. He was safe in a town and off the trail, had clean clothes, was clean himself, had a belly full of beans, a job he did better than most wherever you go, and a pocket full of small change for the start of a stake. Good enough doings, thievery and all.

There was a man—a dashing young sport used to play the wheel and the ladies in San Francisco and points east, used to shoot men kicking for looking cross-eyed—there was this young man would have thought it all sad pickin's.

Old days—old ways.

CHAPTER 3

THE LUNCH-TIME rush finally petered out. It beat Link
why MacDuff got such a good crowd, serving a poor
free lunch as he did. Likely, the other saloons in Colt
Creek did even less proud with it. He washed his sink-
full of mugs and glasses, whipping up a suds with his
bar-rag, giving then a scrub and a rinse and a rinse
again. Out of the corner of his eye he could see young
Parker trying to copy him, doing a better job of
washing-up than he usually did, Link thought. Boy
had something to learn about it, that was sure.

MacDuff came elbowing through the thinning
crowd and up to the bar. "Well, now," he said. "You
do know your business; I'll say that." *Better than you
know yours*, Link thought. "Nice work . . . nice
work." What do you say, Parker?".

"Oh, he's real smooth, Mr. Macuff." Praise from a
master. Link remembered a man he had worked for in
Denver years before, a fat German named Ditters. Mr.
Ditters, now, would have faulted Link's serving up
one side and down the other and caught him palming
to boot. Ditters had known his business. Hadn't been
put off by Link's reputation with a gun, either. Had
paid that no mind at all. With Ditters, you either did

32

your job A-1, or you were out. They would no more have put out a thin lunch-spread at the Silver Mine than they would have let a drunk piss on the bar rail.

Well, beggars weren't much for choosers. He was lucky to have landed what he had. "Thanks for those kind words, Mister MacDuff." That ought to be enough of a butt-kiss for him.

Once he'd mopped the duck-boards (Parker had begged off early, already asking Link could he go tend his Ma, rather than checking with MacDuff) Link went out back to the necessary, got rid of some bean-gas, and pulled on his smoke stained buckskin jacket. Might as well pay up the livery out of the palmed change. There'd be plenty more where that had come from.

He nodded to the old Chinese cook, and went out the back way. He'd seen most of Main Street. Might do to take a look at the side streets, see the town. Must be a whorehouse or two—probably not for him. Cost too damn much, for a start, and sporting people had sharp noses, and long memories. He'd been marked by whores and gay-girls before this. The gay life was a family from San Francisco to New York City, and on over to Europe, for that matter—the girls and pimps, madams and sharpers, the racing people and hooligans. It was a big family, and sooner or later, you'd meet one you knew or they'd know you. Best to stay away from whorehouses. A madam had called him "Frank" not a year ago, in a Wyoming barrel-house as black as the pit. She'd picked him out for Buckskin Frank Leslie as soon as she'd laid eyes on him. Known him in Salt Lake. Had lost a girl to him, in fact, years and years ago.

Was a day he went to the whores regardless, and if there was trouble, or they marked him, so much the worse for them. Now, though, he didn't care for trouble. Tired of it. Just plain tired of it.

The town was quieter now than it had been in the early morning. Must be the Spring roundups bringing drovers and stockmen into town in the mornings for supplies, and a few last drinks before the big jobs started. It seemed to Link that it was still early, up here in the high country, to be bringing the herds in, but maybe not too early to be getting ready for it. In a week or so, Colt Creek would be a ghost town, at least on weekdays. Saturdays, somehow, the drovers would manage to get into town for whiskey and a screw if they had any wages left after bunkhouse poker.

He walked up a muddy side street a block down from the White Rose. There were some shops here, a saddlery and a place selling yard goods and sundries. Link crossed the street and climbed the steps up to the boardwalk. There was still a hard, cold wind blowing down from the mountains, but the sun had warmed the muddy streets into a soft churned-up stew of mud, garbage, and horse manure. It clotted on his boots, smearing them almost to the tops. The high board sidewalks were a climb up and down at each crossing, but it was worth it to stay clear of the mud.

Two women, out shopping, passed him on the boardwalk; they glanced over their shoulders at him as they went by with baskets on their arms. Respectable women in long, dark dresses. Clerk's wives—no, the feathers in their hats were too fancy for that. Banker's wives, or feed merchants'. They hadn't seemed mighty impressed by Link. Odd, how vanity stays with you. Had been a day, and not so long ago, either, when he'd been considered quite the slicker. The last few years had taken some of the slick off him. Taken a lot of it, for good. And the scar down his cheek didn't help. Ladies could like a scar if it wasn't too ugly. This one was—long down his cheek, pink, puckered in the biting cold. "It'll fade," the doctor had said, sewing away in that sunny room. "It'll fade in time."

Well, time had come and gone, a long time past that sunny room in the big, beautiful resort hotel, a pleasure palace in very truth with a princess to match it. Gone now, long gone as far as he was concerned. What a fine draw that little fellow had had. Shannon, he'd called himself. Blond little man, going grey. Wore buckskins, too, and a belt with silver conchos on it. Big, nickel-plated Peacemaker. Wore his revolver high—good a way as any, and better than most—and had that fine fast rolling draw . . .

Good enough to brand Buckskin Frank Leslie's cheek. Word was the little man had killed Slim Wilson, out of Cheyenne. Could be, with a fast draw like that.

Well, the ladies didn't like ugly scars, at least, not on torn-trouser drifters with nothing fine about them but their gun.

Link walked past the saddlery—had no use for a fine saddle unless he got a fine horse to wear it. The old Brazos double-rig the brown sported now was a comfortable seat; Link didn't intend to be roping any wild steers off it. He strolled up by a hardware store, and stopped to look in the big plate glass window. Must have cost a bright penny to freight that glass over the mountains. Link liked to look at hardware—didn't know of a man who didn't, shoe-clerk, or newspaper editor, or whatever. Something satisfying about hardware goods. Made a man feel he might just step in and buy some pretty tools and go build a cabin, or say the hell with it and go out to the coast and build a boat. The tools and time, was all it would take . . .

He walked on up to Main Street and saw that it was as empty as the side street had been. He saw the livery sign across it and a block further down. A white arrow was painted on the bottom of the sign, pointing south, around that corner.

Link walked—waded, some might say—across Main, hurrying a little to get clear of a four-horse dray, about the only traffic there was. Just as he got clear, a horseman on a big pinto spurred out past the wagon and came close to clipping Link as he went by. The rider was a fat boy in a red-spotted shirt. Young as he was, he had a double chin like a railroad man. He called back as he rode, "Hey, Dad! You better trot!" and rode on his way.

Link noticed the fat boy'd worn two guns. Parrot-grip Colt .38's they looked to be. Double-actions. And in a clumsy looking buscadero rig. Odd get-up, all round.

He climbed the boardwalk steps and walked on down the other side of Main. There were a row of clothes shops—get a new fit-out in one of those soon enough—a pharmacy, and the marshal's office. City Marshal—Colt Creek, written in gold leaf paint on a swinging sign over the door. The building was log, not even rough-sawn plank. Must have been one of the first in town. Marshal's office. Jail.

Link glanced in as he passed. No marshal; a little old man, the jailor, probably, was sweeping up. Unlikely to have trouble, even if the marshal was in town. Link wasn't wanted for any crime he knew about, though some law officers would perhaps enjoy to talk with him. He had been wanted, and more than once, but for nothing that would interest anyone now. A pimping charge in Galveston, gambling fines. Nothing for the killings. No lawman had ever arrested him for murder. Or, if any had had the idea, they'd thought better of it. Just as well, too. Link had heard what prison had done to Wes Hardin. Pinched the balls right off him, it was said. Hard to believe of that man, but it was what they said. Link had no intention of ever going to prison. The officer who tried to put him there would be a dead man, that was all. And if Link was dead shortly thereafter, so much the better. No prison; that was that.

Lawmen seemed to sense it about him. Police had come into saloons and dens he was working and hauled a load of grifters and loafers away, and not thought twice about it. But they'd come to Link—didn't look any different from the others, plenty of the others carried pistols—and they'd just shy away. Their glances just passed over him as if he weren't there. And they'd go on their way, and leave him alone. They had a feeling about it, probably.

He came to the corner, turned it, and passed a lumber yard. Some men were outside, stacking sawn planks in the cold. Link remembered the planks dropped alongside the White Rose. This was a building town, no doubt about it, a rich little town as cow-towns went. All the mountain states were doing better than in the south. They'd long since winter-fed their stock with wagoned hay, and it had helped to save them when the big winter had come two years before. Down in Texas, the cattlemen hadn't been so lucky. Link had been there working as a drover, god help him, and had seen the dead beeves piled up in the snowdrifts like cord-wood. That winter had broken some pretty big men, down in Texas.

The big doors to the livery were swung shut, and Link thumped on them with his fists. No answer. He tried them, and they swung slowly open. The Beanpole's office was dark; boss must be home for an after-dinner nap.

Link thought the stable girl had showed enough sense to hold on to some change. He'd pay her for two days, let her hand it to her boss.

He walked into the stable yard, and called out for her. "Yo! Hostler!" Not a peep. He walked on into the stable, down the long dark center aisle. It struck Link, not for the first time, how like a church a stable was, the way it was laid out. There was nobody about, just two long rows of horses' heads in the dimness, nodding, chewing on their feed, couple of them cribbing, worrying at the top of the stall doors with their teeth. He couldn't make out the brown. If the girl hadn't fomented that leg, then he'd have to do it. He couldn't afford a crippled horse. A crippled horse meant you had to steal another, if leaving town was sudden. *Then*, by God, he'd be wanted by the law, that's for damn sure.

He went on down the aisle, looking for the brown, and found him next stall to the last on the left. A white feed-sack bandage shone in the shadows; Link could smell the hot mash. The girl had done her job, all right. The brown, as usual, made no sign of knowing him. A near-useless horse. The best of them were boneheads; when you came on an exceptionally stupid one, you were thankful if he remembered to neck rein.

Link started to open the stall door to check the water bucket. Might as well see the beast settled in since he'd come down here—then he heard something strange.

Crying? Something. Link stood quiet, listening. After a few moments, it came again. Clearer, this time; sounded like that stable girl. The sound came from the loft. Crying, or groaning. Poor thing had enough to be sorry about, likely.

He reached for the stall door again and heard two men laughing just before he touched it. The girl groaned again.

Link stood still in the stable shadows.

The men laughed again. There was a slapping, smacking sound, and the girl cried out.

Link was at the base of the steep loft ladder before he thought. Then he stopped. *None of my put-in—None of my God-damned business. They won't kill her. Stay out of it!*

He climbed the ladder.

He kept as quiet as he could. It was a long climb; the loft was almost two full storeys high. Hay dust clouded around him as he climbed up through the shadows; the smell of hay was rich around him. His boots scraped a little on the rungs.

He eased up through the bale hatch slowly and carefully. The loft was wide and long, with a ceiling beamed like a sailing ship. From a distant small window, from chinks in the rough cedar shakes above, pale beams of sunlight streamed down here and there. Dust motes drifted in them.

Three men had the girl down. One was standing against a wall of bales, watching. That was two more men than Link had counted on, and the man watching had a revolver stuck in his belt. But he wasn't a gunman. Neither were the men on the girl. They looked to be roughs—laborers, and most likely from the lumberyard nearby.

They had stripped the girl naked, except for a pair of wool stockings, men's socks they looked like, down around her ankles. One of the men was naked except for his shirt, a short, muscular red-headed man. The other two had taken off their trousers. The red-headed man was kneeling in the hay beside the girl's head, holding her shoulders down. The girl was whimperng, making strained gobbling noises in her throat. The other two men were at her, one squeezing and tugging at her small pointed breasts, pulling at the nipples, pinching them. His cock stuck out from under his shirt-tails, stiff, inflamed. The other man had gotten on top of her, wedged his thigh between her skinny narrow ones, and forced one of her long slim legs up and out, spreading her. Her skin was paper-white. There was only a faint patch of brown hair at her crotch. The man who'd spread her had his hand on it, working at her, getting his fingers into her.

The girl gobbled again and whined, kicking out with her free leg. Thin ridges of muscle moved under her white skin as she struggled; she was leaned down to bone and muscle from all the stable work, there was no woman-fat on her at all. Sweat shone on her skin as she struggled in their hands.

Link had two choices—butt in or butt out. And either choice would cost him. He could drive these people off; they wouldn't be much to handle. But he would be a marked man once he'd done it. The story would get around; these men would carry their grudges at being roughly handled. Link would be labeled a hard-case, at least a small-time one.

On the other hand, he could ease back down the damn ladder and stay out of it. It would be the smart thing to do, the wise thing to do.

You're too damn old—too damn worn out for this.

The man pulling at the girl's nipples pinched her harder, tugged at her. The girl twisted in the straw, cried out in that strangled bird's cry; a thin white arm pushed at him.

Link came up out of the hay hatch without a sound, stood crouched in the shadowed gloom, and then began slowly to work his way to the right, past a long pile of stacked bales. The man with the revolver was leaning against that stack more than thirty feet away, still watching what was being done to the half-witted girl, one hand massaging himself, squeezing at his genitals through his trousers as he watched.

Link moved in behind the wall of hay. No gunplay —no damn gunplay if he could help it! He reached down to the top of his right boot, found the end of the toothpick's handle, and drew the knife. A five-inch walnut grip and seven slim inches of needle-pointed, razor-sharp, double-edged blade. A beauty, cold-ground under ice water out of a fine broad file. Whenever his straight razor lost its set, Link shaved with the knife. It shaved as smooth as grease on glass, but the length of the blade made it too tricky for the fine work along the upper lip. A good mustache came in handy if you shaved with a killing knife. That was what the Arkansas toothpick was really for. Wasn't much use as a camp knife.

Link had known men who so prided themselves on their knife-fighting that they didn't even carry a gun. He thought those men were fools. He'd killed only four men with a knife in his life—two with this blade— and he'd wished devoutly for a loaded revolver on each occasion.

The girl was grunting now, her voice muffled. Link listened to that, and to the muttered voices of the men as he stepped carefully through the deep, loose hay behind the long stack of bales. He sure as hell didn't need to step into another loading hatch and drop ass over tea-kettle into the stable below.

A few more steps and he reached the break in the haystack. The bound bales had fallen loose here, and through the dusty gloom, Link saw the right shoulder of the watching man. He was wearing a blue checked shirt. The material of the shoulder moved rythmically as he stroked himself. Link could hear his breathing, the sounds the other men made with the girl. Her whimpers . . . hoarse whispers . . . the soft slap of flesh on flesh.

Link stepped over a wide, loose bale, leaned in

41

against the watching man's shoulder, and brought the toothpick around in a quick, smooth arc. He sliced the tip of the man's nose off—just the last little fraction of an inch of it.

The watching man froze stock still in shock. A small jet of blood, bright scarlet in a beam of sunlight, spattered down his shirt. When he drew in air with a gasp to yell, Link put the edge of the knife against his throat, and moved it, slid it just the least bit to one side. He felt the man's skin tug very slightly, and start to part.

"Don't make a sound," he said softly into the man's ear. "One squeal out of you, and I'm going to cut your throat." He said it in a reasonable tone of voice, as if it were a promise, a casual committment in a trade of some kind.

The watching man wasn't watching any more. His body shook hard against Link's where they leaned together. His cut nose was dripping steadily, ruining his shirt. His eyes were tight closed, like a frightened child's.

Link reached across and down to pull the fellow's revolver out of his belt. It felt like one of the old Confederate Whitneys. As he tossed it behind him into the hay, Link glanced at the other men. They'd noticed nothing, intent on the girl. She was still writhing, still struggling under them. The red-headed man still knelt at her shoulders; the man at her meagre breasts was nuzzling them now, sucking at her nipples, biting at them as she twisted in the sun-spotted hay. The third man had her split and spraddled, the long, thin, white legs spread wide. He had fingers deep into her; Link saw the wet of her gash bright pink around the shoving, working fingers. The man was over her, hunching, his cock stiff in his other hand.

"Hold still—hold still, you bitch!" His voice was

42

hoarse, thick with wanting.

"*You* hold still, Dog-ass!" Link said. The instant he said it, he saw the lean girl turn desperately in the soft carpet of hay and, the tendons and veins of her slender throat standing in bold relief, manage to stretch an avid mouth up to the red-headed man's erect cock, lick at it, and, throat still painfully arched, began to suckle on it like a starving baby. She grunted in satisfaction.

Like men waking from a dream, the three of them turned to stare up at Link, their hands still on her.

It was a strange moment for it, but Link felt as shamed and embarrassed as he could ever remember feeling. Not that he had mistaken the poor girl's animal heat and the men at it with her, for a rough rape. But that it was such a perfect reward for his interfering at all.

The hero. The big-time gunman showing the roughs. Saving a half-wit girl. *The hero*. How Holliday would have laughed. "Frank," he would have said, "You have revived my faith in human nature!" He would have laughed about it for a month, laughing that dry, creaky laugh of his. "Absolutely revived my faith!"

"God damn you," the red-headed man said. He looked mad as fire. "What have you done to Willy? You've cut him, damn you!" And he was on his feet and coming for Link on the jump.

Too many of them. Too many for even a "hero" to fist-fight. And god knew Link couldn't shoot them down, not for his own stupidity. And way too late to bow out gracefully and leave them to it. Christ, he'd sliced this poor fool in the blue checked shirt to a fare-thee-well. He'd have to push it through—and all his own damn fault!

The red-headed man came swinging—looked strong as a horse—Link ducked and dodged away, took a punch on his shoulder that knocked a grunt out of him, and came back with the toothpick. He swung the blade up at the redhead's naked belly. The blade flashed in a gold ribbon of sunlight. The redhead put his hands down to stop it, and Link windmilled the knife down, away, and back up and around overhand, like a baseball pitch, turned his wrist to reverse the knife, and struck the man in the forehead with the butt. It was a sharp, hard, whacking sound, and the red-headed man made an odd springing jump and fell over against the bales, his right foot kicking spasmodically. Link hit him again, on the side of the head, just missing the temple. The man made an odd "oooohh" noise, and slid down to sit in the hay.

The other two men had had to hold a moment to pull up their pants. The red-head was down by then. Link had long ago learned not to let men catch their breath in a fight. He jumped at the two of them, flourishing the toothpick. They stepped back. He drew the Bisley, and cocked it.

The watching-man was behind him, now, but Link heard him crying and dabbing at his nose, and was content to leave him there.

The two men in front of him watched the gun, and they watched his face. "Take your friends and get out. You bother my little girl again, I'll kill you."

Good enough. Sounded enough like her daddy or some relative, to make them think.

The two men hesitated, glanced at each other then back to Link and the Bisley Colt's.

One of them, a man with a long jaw, and a nose to match it, cleared his throat and spoke up, his eyes still on Link's gun. "Now, looky here, Mister—now, now we didn't know . . ."

"Shut up," Link said, "you son-of-a-bitch." He let

his voice rise, and lifted the Colt's muzzle to meet their eyes.

"Say, Nate," the other man said. "Listen now, I think we better get on out of this." Nate didn't say anything.

"Take your friends, and clear out."

"All right," the man called Nate said. "All right; we ain't looking for any trouble with you or the girl, Mister." He eyed the gun and the knife, and slowly bent to help the red-headed man to his feet. The redhead could stand, but he didn't seem to know what had happened. He stood swaying, blinking his eyes in a bright beam of sunlight. There was no blood on his head.

Nate started leading him back the way Link had come, back toward the loft ladder. "Tarnation," the other man said, "Bill's buck-naked, Nate!"

"Then bring his damn clothes!" Nate didn't appear to want to linger. The other man kicked through the hay, found the piled clothing, and came back to take the crying man by the arm and lead him off with the others.

Link watched them go, two wading along through the thick hay, supporting their friends. When they got to the loading hatch, the one called Nate turned to say something over his shoulder, braver now that the violence was over.

"What did you say?" Link called to him. He could see the man's pale face in the loft shadows.

"I said, you had no call to be so rough, Mister! We're not bad fellas. We work for our living same as you do, I'll bet. We had none of us no notion at all this girl had any family but old Perry, and he don't mind."

"You better get," Link said. The man stopped talking, and pushed the man with the cut nose down onto the ladder and climbed after him in some haste. The red-headed man had been the stud duck in that fit-out.

Link stood, listening as the men climbed down the ladder. He heard some murmurs down in the stable and a sudden loud angry voice. Red had woken up, doubtless looked to climb back up and continue the fight. Link listened to the muffled argument below, and gradually it seemed funnier and funnier to him—not just that sharp sport, Frank Leslie, stepping in like one of Ned Buntline's imaginary sap-heads, to rescue a poor half-witted girl who'd be happier in a cash-house than feeding horses, but the whole thing—the poor devil with a bit of his nose cut clean off and the others with their pants down . . . Link couldn't help himself; he started to giggle like a dressmaking sissy, trying to stop, or at least keep from laughing out loud. That would sure as hell bring those boys back up, mad as fire!

He wiped the toothpick's blade on a hay bale, and bent to slide it into his boot, keeping his mouth closed on his laughter so that he snorted through his nose trying not to roar out loud. Knowing he had to be quiet just made it worse. And every mutter from downstairs started it all over again. His belly was hurting with it.

Then he heard them marching off down there, out into the stable yard. He could hear a high, complaining voice. That would be the fellow with the cut nose. *"Nez Coupe,"* the French trappers would say.

Link leaned back into the bales and let loose. He threw his head back and laughed the way he hadn't laughed in years. Not in years. He laughed until he was exhausted, the sound of his laughter ringing around the loft's vaulted roof, and finally subsided into groans, sighs.

What a piece of jackassery! And by God, he felt the better for it! He felt fine. He'd have to buy those boys a drink!

A rustling in the hay. Link had forgotten the girl, in all this hooray. She hadn't moved. Hadn't tried to cover herself.

CHAPTER 4

SHE LAY naked, spreadeagled in the hay, her narrow belly, still wet with the sweat of struggle, shining white under a beam of sunlight from the old roof above. Her eyes were in shadow, but Link could see them on him, eyes as blue, as blank, as a summer day. Thin-lipped, her face bony, hollow-cheeked, she lay outstretched as lean as a racing dog, every slight muscle and taut tendon showing.

She made again that soft moaning sound he had first heard below, by the lame brown's stall. She moaned, and moved slightly in the straw, doubling one long, thin leg, folding it at the knee and letting it fall away again. It revealed her secret, the dab of wet hair—darker brown than the tangled hair that lay beneath her head like a wild-fringed pillow—and a wet, slight line of pink, her gash's mark within the fur.

Then, as Link stood looking down at her, the girl reached slowly down, and touching herself tenderly with the long fingers of both hands, slowly, delicately pulled herself open for him to see.

The pink sank to purple in that split; the small hole stretched by her fingers showed her soaking in deep delicate folds. Her finger tips were oily with herself;

48

the wet plastered down the hairs at her crotch. She tugged at herself, spreading the lips wide as a butterfly's wings, orange-red, glistening.

Link stared down at her. It had been a long time . . . Not since a fat Indian whore in Butte, two weeks before . . .

But not this way. Not with a poor half-wit girl. Not much better than screwing some animal, for all she knew or cared. And the leavings of those four fools, as well.

Not this way.

The girl stared up at him for a moment longer, then she closed her eyes, and turned her head away, still gripping herself, spreading herself for him.

That she had done that, closed her eyes, made some odd and powerful difference to him. It made things seem all right; it made it seem to be cruel, were he to walk away through the hay, now, and leave her there, her offering rejected.

He felt his cock stiffen in his trousers as he watched her, and his heart was pounding like some boy's in his first whorehouse parlor.

Then, he didn't care what she was. He only cared for what he saw; the long, thin legs, naked, scratched and stable-bruised; the smooth, white, thin-ribbed length of her; the thick thumbs of her nipples rising from meagre breasts; shadowed air-pits, the hollows at her thin throat, no bigger around than a child's; long, slight, wire-muscled arms—and, at her center, under her hands, that open wound.

Link no longer gave a damn. He didn't worry about interruption; God help the man who came up into this loft. He saw something he wanted and that wanted him.

He unbuckled his gun belt and let it fall to the broken bale behind him; he bent and shucked his boots and socks. Then, still watching the girl who lay silent, her head turned away, her eyes closed, her long fingers gently working at her groin, he stripped off his shirt, trousers and long-johns, and, his stiff cock swaying before him, stepped through the soft hay to her.

He stood above her, smelling her rank, foxy smell. The stink of the stable was on her, and the fish-glue stink of unwashed girl. She did not turn her head to look up at him. She lay still, except for those gently working fingers.

Link knelt, gripped her wrists, and slowly pulled her thin hands away. She lay completely still then, exposed to him.

He put his hands on her slim thighs, slowly bent his head and began to lick at her. Began to lick that weeping gash as delicately, as steadily, as a hungry cat.

The girl tasted rich, and sweet, and soft, and rotten as a spoiled spring. Link drank deep, using his lips, his tongue, his nose, to burrow into her wetness. He began to eat her as if he were famished, had been dying of hunger, for just this. The girl began to whimper like a puppy; the long, thin legs shifted restlessly, sliding along Link's sides. As he bent, working at her. She began to buck up to him, throwing her thighs wide, thrusting her groin up to his mouth. Thin, work-hardened hands came wandering down to grip Link's hair, to hold his head hard against her. When he began to bite her gently, worrying the slippery, soft meat with his teeth, her whimpers slowly grew louder, until she was talking, or trying to talk, crying out in an odd, nasal voice. She was calling for her mother: "Mommy" was the only word he could understand.

Link needed more than he was getting. He pulled away from her, away from the clutching hands and reached forward to grip her at the nape of her neck with one hand, while the other placed his cock to her, feeling the damp heat against the tip. She thrashed, wanting it or fearing it, trying to get away.

Link held her hard at the back of the neck, knelt on one of her thighs to hold her still, found her again with his cock, and slowly, steadily, drove deep, deep into her.

She gripped him like a hot, wet fist, squeezing along the length of his rod as it rode into her. He almost lost his jissom to her then, gasping with the pleasure of it, his arms shaking as he supported himself above her. His cock made a wet, juicy sound as it went in. The girl, silent now, began a slow, twisting, writhing movement beneath him—almost a kind of dance as she screwed herself up onto his cock. Her long, thin legs were wrapped around him now as tight as baling twine, her hard, small hands gripped the muscles of his arms so strongly they hurt him.

Her long horse-face was expressionless, blank. Those vacant blue eyes stared up at him as blind as any statue's. Only the ceaseless snapping, twisting movement of her narrow hips, the quick wet sounds of her as his cock rode in and out, showed any passion. She might have been dreaming of something else entirely except for the dripping gash that moved desperately beneath him.

For a short while, there was no sound in the loft but the rhythmic rustle of crushed hay and their hoarse breathing as they labored against each other.

Then, as Link began to lose control, began to feel the aching surge of pleasure build and build, something happened to the girl.

Her slim, strong hands, that had been scratching, clutching at him suddenly began to beat frantically on the muscle of his back. Her legs began to kick out in desperate, thrusting spasms, and the thin latigo-tough body suddenly writhed and bucked beneath him, slamming up into him as if she were trying to hurl him off of her.

Too late for that.

Link snarled down at her, and reached up to grip her hair, to hold her down while he finished. He hunched up and into her, harder and harder—bearing down, bearing down. Her coozy squeezed around him, hard enough to hurt.

He didn't care. He didn't care that she began to wail, an odd, keening note that went on and on. His cock felt huge, swollen, ready to burst, to flood out, to take him all away on the flood.

And he came. As the girl made a strangling, spitting noise in her throat, and convulsed under him.

Link reared back on stiffened arms, groaning with the pleasure of it, letting it go. Letting it all go. He felt at that moment, as he always did then, that he loved the girl—for her beauty . . . for the great gift of pleasure she had given him.

Then he looked down.

The girl was in convulsions. The empty blue eyes rolled back up into her head, streaks of bloody foam running from her mouth. She was biting her tongue to pieces.

"Christ!" Link jammed the heel of his hand between her champing jaws, and she bit him to the bone. He felt a flood of warmth down his thigh; the poor damn thing was pissing on him. He rolled off her, and out of her, with a last slippery pleasure, still holding his hand wedged in her mouth. She was deep in her brainstorm, her eyes up out of sight under fluttering lids, blood— some of it his—spattering from her mouth, snorting and snoring as if she couldn't catch her breath. Her legs doubled at the knees and kicked out again and again.

Link, stark naked, fresh come and fresh pissed-on, kept his hand where it was. It could take more biting than the kid's tongue, for sure, and it was his left hand, anyway—and otherwise tried to keep her from thrashing so savagely she might throw a joint out in her legs or arms.

He'd seen an old drover do just that with the jumps from lockjaw, and these convulsions looked near as bad.

It went on for a weary time.

Then maybe five minutes after the epilepsy began, Link could see that the convulsions were slowly becoming less severe, less violent. In the next few minutes, the girl gradually became quieter, finally lying almost still, her legs and arms quivering as if she'd been shot, but not contorting as they had been.

It was an almighty relief to Link who'd had visions of himself, still pulling up his pants, running out onto the street calling for some damn doctor to come to her. He tugged his aching hand free of the girl's clenched teeth and examined the bite; it was a sight. He kept on soothing the girl, talking to the poor thing the way a man would to a sick horse. After a bit, the girl groaned and opened her eyes. Link tried to keep her lying down, but she got anxious and struggled up—and vomited right away, her thin shoulders heaving, her face red with strain as she upchucked what looked to be a considerable breakfast.

None of that got on Link, for a change.

When she was done, he got his arms underneath her, lifted her, and carried her over to a pile of fresh hay against the loft wall. He settled her there, and took the chance of climbing down the loft ladder, naked, and trotting out into the stableyard to the pump and troughs. He didn't wait to pump himself any fresh. He just tipped up, ass-over-teakettle, and rolled

53

into a full trough of icy water and wallowed in it, puffing and blowing. Then he was up and out, trotted back into the stable for a bucket, came back out and scooped some water up, and toted that, sloshing, up the loft ladder into the warm hay now. He found the girl's shirt, and while she submitted as docile as a lady's dog, he mopped her clean.

Then, and with a great deal of relief, he dried himself with his shirt and put his clothes on, socks and boots, and buckled on his revolver. The girl, dull-eyed and still as ever, had lain watching him as he dressed, and combed the hay-stems out of his hair with his fingers.

"How're you feeling, honey?"

She watched him, and made a sound in her throat.

"Better?" It was only a guess at what she'd said, but the girl nodded, and then went back to staring, dumb as a range cow.

"Well, you rest up here 'till you feel all right, you hear?" Just lay there, looking. "I'll get a horse blanket from below there . . ."

He stayed on a bit more time, what with fetching the horse blanket and putting that over her and noticing she was happy to drink the trough-water. He asked her if she knew she'd had a fit. Some people who had them didn't even know it, he'd heard. But she did; at the word "fit," she'd moaned and nodded.

Then he'd said "Doctor . . . *Doc* . . ." to her, but she hadn't appeared to get that at all. Still, she looked a lot easier. Seemed to be well enough, considering.

He'd stayed around longer than he should have, probably, considering that Beanpole who owned the livery was some kind of relative to her. Didn't need a dust-up with that fellow, on top of almost taking the nose clear off the loafer. Still, he stayed around for a while longer, just to make sure she wasn't going to have another fit right away, and end up swallowing her tongue or something.

It was a relief to be out of it.

He walked out through the stable yard; the dusty windows still showed Beanpole's office empty. Link felt mighty damn odd, all in all—shakey, for one thing, from the toughest, sweetest screwing . . . and with an idiot girl, too. One who fell into a fit over it! Nothing much to be proud of there, to be tupping at a poor idiot girl who didn't know any better, had no idea of decent behavior. Nice doings for Mister Frank Leslie, of San Francisco and points east. *That* fine gent—*that* dashing sport. Fine doings.

He'd be fucking a sheep next.

And in trouble because of this start. The redheaded man wouldn't forget being buffaloed. He and his friends would be on the lookout for a busybody with a knife and a Bisley Colt's.

Well, he could have minded his own business, starting with the first groan out of her, coming down from the hay loft. Could have minded his own business—watered the brown, checked the dressing, and gotten the hell out and back to the White Rose. Getting time for the dinner rush, anyway.

He turned up Main Street. Still no crowd to buck; the round-ups must be on, right enough. He walked along the high board sidewalk toward the Rose, his boot-steps echoing down the planking. Warmer, now, than it had been this morning, but whether from the screwing, or the girl's sickness after that, or just plain trail-weariness, he was feeling tired out. Bird-frail, and dog-tired. It would be good to climb into the soogins tonight, get that herder's stove red hot, have a belly full of the Chink's cooking, and climb into those blankets for a long night's sleep.

There was a day he'd have done his stint

bartending, quit at three in the morning, played some cards 'till dawn—then, flush or on tick, strolled to the best house in town and ordered up a tired, sleepy whore. And, by God, he'd have whiskeyed and cashed and spanked and fucked her up to a fare-thee-well! And the Lord save any man who'd gotten in his way.

Was a day . . .

No more. Not any more. Here he was, just a wore out citizen yearning for beddy-bye.

Parker was already working when Link stepped through the swinging doors, serving beer to a row of drummers. Link asked after the boy's mother as he slid in behind the bar, and that loosened the boy's reins somewhat. He gave Link a smile, and a "good evening Mister Link," and a considerable report on his mother's health. Mrs. Parker, who, it seemed, had enjoyed perfect health up to four years ago, had suddenly gone into a hard decline. A patch on the liver, the doctor said, and it had sent her to her bed. Only Parker to care for her. Had a sister, married to a railroad man. Never cared about their mother, no help whatsoever. It was all up to him. And he was glad to do it. No man, no real man, but would do his absolute possible for his mother.

The drummers—two in rope-and-line, one a Glidden man with hook-wire samples right here in his case, the other a traveler for Staley—Whitford revolvers, out of Pittsfield, Mass.—all agreed. It was a sign of a man, that his mother came first with him. Where would he be without her? "Still an angel," one of the drummers said, the one in rope-in-line. "Say," he said, "I could use a hauling; I hear you have some redskin girls out here will lick your whatever for a dollar even. That true?"

Parker flushed so his pimples glowed. "I wouldn't know," he said. The change of subject had been too

56

abrupt for him. "New in town, myself," Link said, "but I wouldn't be surprised."

"Those damn red niggers," the Glidden man said, wiggling a finger for another beer. "Those red niggers killed my whole family, all of my uncle's people, anyway. In Texas." He was a very small, thin man, with an orange-tipped drinker's nose. "Come to think about it," he said. "I believe my aunt is still a captive out there." He winked. "Draggin' some Commanche's ashes for him, you bet."

There was general agreement that Indians were hell on white women. Whiskey and white women—the Indians were made for them. "Hell, I'm mad for 'em myself," said the Glidden man, to general agreement.

It was the sort of nonsense that a good bartender could listen to, and answer, by the hour, and pay no real heed to any of it. Link had long ago learned that most men went to saloons because they were lonesome. The drinking was only the excuse for the visit.

Soon, as the bar crowded up, Link left the drummers to Parker, and began serving the other end, a noisy ocean-breaker of drovers and stock chousers from the yards outside of town. He saw how MacDuff managed his profit, even during round-up. The men from the stockyards were a steady line of customers, no matter what, and there'd always be drovers coming into the pens from the range, bringing in the beef, and stealing a half hour from the foreman to down a beer in Colt Creek.

It explained MacDuff's poor free-lunch as well. Stockyard workers could carve a steak from a broke-leg cripple after almost any fast loading. Link had often seen them, dirty-faced, burly men, crouching by their hooches along the yard-fencing, roasting thick, dangling cow steaks over brushwood fires. Not much interest in free lunch among easy feeders like those.

57

It made for a coarse crowd, by and large. Cheap chuck-a-luck gamblers. Link could see the big wheels spinning in the back of the wide room—not much high-rolling from this crowd. Still, there was bound to be a high-stake game. Bound to be some big-timers— big for the town, anyway—who liked a high-stake game, who found a pleasure in taking chances with what they owned. Careful chances, to be sure.

Link served out four beers to as many yard men. Could tell them by the smell as well as their beef-fed faces. He palmed a two-bit piece, rattled the rest into the cash box, and pocketed the coin as he turned away. Good pickin's in Rubeville.

It was a long night, just the same.

That little fight in the hay loft—and the girl, after-ward—had taken a lot out of him. Still trail-tired. At not even midnight, Link was longing for that narrow cot in the liquor room. Trouble was the last thing on his mind.

Just after midnight, Link was down at his end of the bar; he had just finished pouring a small measure of rye over the deep bite the girl had given him on the heel of his left hand. He'd seen plenty of men have trouble with bites they'd gotten from people, one way or another. He clenched and unclenched his hand under the serving counter, pouring more red-eye over the toothmarks. It burned like fire, bit into him, just where she had. Damned little animal! She should be up and over her fit by now, back to caring for the stock.

He heard Parker saying something up the bar, over the noise of the customers. "Come on, now, fella. Come on now . . ." Link knew that tone of voice. He reached under the bar for a bung-starter, and then casually wiped his way up the shining mahogany to where the trouble was. *Keep it short and simple, now*

. . . and for the love of God, no damn gunplay!

Parker was leaning over the bar, talking earnestly to a tall, bony drover with a long red face and combed out black Burnside Whiskers. He was better dressed than the run of cowpokers, with a necktie and a fancy striped shirt. He was grinning at what Parker was saying to him. One of the fat little whores was on his other side. Link could see how the drover's fingers were pressed deep into the soft white flesh of her right arm.

"Now," the drover said—he had a Canadian's Scotch burr—"now, I'll call this fat split-tail anything I please to call her." The girl was slack-faced, trembling. The drover's long fingers squeezed harder into her soft upper arm. "I'll call a deef-and-dummy whatsoever I choose—"

"We don't want trouble here," Parker said. He glanced for support at the men listening at the bar, on either side of the red-faced drover. But they were just watching.

The fat girl began to cry. Huge shining tears began to run down her cheeks. Her dark eyes were wide, like a frightened child's.

"Oh, dear," the drover said, mimicking Parker. He twisted harder at the girl's arm. "Oh, deary me . . . We don't want trouble!"

Link saw that the man wore a long-barreled Peacemaker in a deep-pocket range holster. A good rig for riding and working, but too slow in a fight. He wiped his way up the bar to a place almost across from the drover, a foot or two down from where Parker was standing. The drover glanced over at him, but Link had his head down, was busy wiping.

When the drover's eyes left him, Link brought the bung-starter up from beneath the bar shelf, dropped the bar-rag, and, gripping the oak starter with both hands, as if it were a baseball bat, he swung it as hard as he could and hit the drover across the ear with it.

The sharp cracking sound echoed across the saloon, and silenced a lot of noise.

The drover, still gripping the girl's arm, fell to his knees at the bar rail. Then, with his free hand, he reached up to grip the bar to haul himself to his feet. Link whirled the bung-starter up in both hands again, and brought it down as hard as he could on the drover's fingers where they curled over the edge of the bar. The noise of this blow was as loud as the first.

Link heard the drover gasp with the pain of his broken fingers, and watched as the man shook his head like an injured horse, and with some trouble, climbed to his feet. He had let go of the girl. He stood up, his eyes squinted with pain, staring at Link. Then he tried to take out his revolver, but the hand he was reaching with was the one with broken fingers. It wouldn't work for him.

As he was trying, Link took another full swing and hit him across the face with the starter. The drover's nose broke and he fell backward full length and lay in the sawdust with his hands up to his face as if he were afraid Link would be hitting him again.

"Any man or lady standing at this bar will be left in peace," Link said, loud enough for the people there to hear him.

Nobody at the bar said anything. They looked at Link, and they looked down at the drover, whose fine shirt was ruined with blood from his broken nose. The drover had rolled onto his stomach, and was trying to get up on all fours.

"Does this man have friends here?" Link asked.

After a moment, a short man, a bow-legged drover with some teeth missing in front and wearing a yellow bandanna, stepped up and said, "I'm a Rockin'-D man. I'll get him on his horse." He pulled the hurt drover up and got him standing, and walked him out through the crowd to the bat-wings.

"Bravo!"

A man had called it from the far end of the bar. Link saw it was Wilson Coe, dressed, as before, like a gentleman. Coe raised his glass in salute. "Neatly done, barkeep." He was smiling in the same friendly way he had that morning.

Link turned away without answering, and went on back down the bar. Young Parker said something to him as he went, but Link didn't pay attention to that either. He was busy going over the whole thing in his head, wondering if he should have done it at all. The deaf-and-dumb girls must be used to being roughly treated. Perhaps there'd been no need to take a hand at all. At least there'd been no killing.

At least there'd been no damned killing . . .

He noticed the looks the men along the bar were giving him. He'd seen those looks before. They held all the satisfaction that men feel on seeing something done that they'd have liked to be able to do. Link had seen that look many times. He was sick to death of it. If he hadn't been so tired, he might have thought twice before knocking that loud drover down. At his end of the bar, he turned to the men standing there, yard men, it seemed, and said, "Well? What'll it be?"

"Beer!" they said all together, just like a church choir, and nodded all together, too, watching him as if he was about to catch on fire. Link drew their beers, paddled and placed them and put all the money in the drawer. Too damn many people staring at him. That bung-starter business was going to cost him money, at this rate.

MacDuff came shouldering through the yardmen, leaned on the bar, and gave Link a hard look. "I didn't hire you as a bully, Mister," he said. "That was a Coe man you just beat over there. Did you know that?"

"He started the trouble." Link said, feeling like a boy caught fighting in the schoolyard. "And Wilson Coe didn't appear troubled by it."

MacDuff stared at him a moment more, then jerked his head toward the stairs. "You come on up to my office, right now." And he turned and shoved his way through the customers.

Link figured maybe his plum job was a thing of the past. And who was to blame for that? A damn fool who put his two cents into every pot that came up, that's who. Christ, and wasn't he old enough to know better? More than old enough. That business at the livery wasn't enough for dashing Frank Leslie, the ladies' champion. Oh, no, not for that fine pimp and gunman! Mister Leslie must be forever proving himself, forever showing off his knacky ways with knives and oak sticks—and revolvers, of course, if it came to that . . .

Quite a fellow, and soon to be back on the trail with a pocket full of greasy two-bit pieces and a lame brown horse. On the trail and with a good two or three weeks to go before Spring really came warm to the high country.

Am I such a little man as all this. Such a poor thing?

He ducked under the trap at this end of the bar, and walked through the crowd after MacDuff. Men shifted out of his way as he came through, and he felt their eyes on him . . . on the Bisley Colt's, too.

A fuss in a kennel, a little snarling and a snap, and the other dogs were wary.

Dog doin's.

CHAPTER 5

MACDUFF'S OFFICE was a little cubby off the street end of the horseshoe balcony over the barroom of the White Rose. Link followed the owner up the stairs, and left, down the bare-board corridor into his office.

The office was nothing to boast about. Most salooners did themselves proud in their digs, fancy velvet curtains, and horse-hair sofas, lace anti-macassers—whorehouse sorts of rooms. Not MacDuff.

Link imagined it was Scotch dearness kept MacDuff from plumping up his nest a little. There was nothing in his office but a plain pine desk and two cane-bottom chairs. There was a picture of a prize fighter tacked up on the wall. A page from the *Police Gazette*, it looked like. Link didn't recognize the fighter.

MacDuff squeezed in behind his desk and sat down with a grunt, motioning Link to the other chair. Then he leaned forward and took the top off a Mason jar on the desk and took out what looked like a Havana cigar, long, big and black as a bear turd. He didn't offer one to Link.

Leaning back in his cane-bottom, MacDuff took his time getting the stogie going, warming it at the flame of an Ohio Blue-tip, licking at it, puffing, and all the rest, all the while giving Link hard looks through the smoke.

Link was beginning to like MacDuff, the way he tended to like all eccentric people who didn't have much harm in them. MacDuff reminded him of a fat Prussian general he had guided on a hunt once. Hunting elk. MacDuff was the same sort of soft-center bluff back of a thin hard-case.

"Now you listen to me, Mister . . ." MacDuff was using the cigar for emphasis, pointing it at Link.

"Link."

"Now, you listen to me, Mister Whatever-your-name-is, I just hired you on this very morning, and damned if you haven't already gone and beaten one of my customers with a damn stick! Well, I won't have it! Do you understand that?" He leaned back in the cane-bottom, which creaked under his weight. It occurred to Link that one day, MacDuff would lean back too far, and once too often. He thought, also, that it didn't sound like MacDuff was firing him off the place.

"Do you understand what I'm saying?"

"The fellow needed to be struck," Link said.

"Not by you, God-dammit! Nor by any man who works for me! Do you know who that drover works for? He works for Anse Coe, that's who!"

Link sat looking at him. That cigar smoke smelled mighty good. It was a sure-enough Havana. MacDuff apparently would spend money on something, if not fine furnishings and straight free-lunch.

MacDuff sat puffing for a while, abstracted, looking past Link and out of the dirty little window over-looking the street. Link could hear a teamster outside yelling his horses through the mud. MacDuff put his Havana down in a cracked dish on the desk, and leaned forward to place all four chair legs on the floor. The chair creaked again when he did it. "Look," he said, "just how long were you planning on staying in this town? If you don't mind my asking."

"A few weeks,' Link said.

"A few weeks . . . Going for a stake, are you?"

"A small one, maybe."

"Not out of my cash drawer, by God?" MacDuff said, giving Link the hardest look he could.

"I'm no thief," Link said. Well, it had been true, once.

MacDuff sighed. "Now, you listen to me—and if you repeat what I say to you, I'll call you a God-damned liar to your face. Understand that?" He waited for Link to say something, and when he didn't, sighed again. "The Coes," he said, "The Coes—and by that I mean, and *everybody* means Charles Jackson Anse Coe—runs this town. Hell, he runs the territory for a hundred miles around."

"There's always somebody," Link said. "What business is this of mine?"

"It may be your business, bartender, because that was one of Anse Coe's men you knocked down with that bung-starter!" He went back to puffing on his stogie. The cigar smoke smelled very fine. "*Mister* Anse Coe owns the Rocking-D, which is the biggest ranch in these parts. He owns most of this town—and I mean lock, stock, and barrel—and," he looked suddenly sad, "the son-of-a-bitch owns exactly fifty-one percent of the White Rose."

Link saw nothing new in any of this. It was a very usual arrangement in boom towns. It explained why MacDuff had let Wilson Coe buffalo him this morning.

"That Coe downstairs . . .?"

"Wilson," MacDuff said, and bit down hard on the Havana. "That damn Yale College sissy! You say I said any of this, and I'll call you a liar, now! That smiling son-of-a-bitch! He's a lawyer—wouldn't you know it? Does old Anse's dirty work in town for him. The old man's nephew. And nothing but a dirty snake in the grass! Man never dirties his hands. Never dirties them! Just sneaks around with 'Mister Coe would appreciate . . .' The son-of-a-bitch!"

It appeared that MacDuff had been carrying a grudge unspoken for some time. "It's none of my put-in," Link said. "But if the Coes weigh too heavy, why not just pick up and go? Plenty of traveling room in this country."

MacDuff grunted, and looked straight at Link without squinting or trying it on tough. "My agreement with the Coes states I stay and run the Rose, period."

Link smiled.

"Yeah, you can laugh up your sleeve, bartender. But let me tell you something: Anse Coe is an old man, but he had them that see his agreements kept." He looked away, biting at his mustache. "There was a man in this town named Cramer, Everett Cramer, and a decenter fellow never drew breath. Cramer had a freight line, ran from here to Boise. A damn good business . . ." MacDuff was speaking so softly now that Link had trouble hearing him. "Coe bought into that freight line—Cramer had no choice about it. And, by God, forced Cramer to agree to stay and manage it! Well . . old Everett just up and ran off! Ran off to Pennsylvania—clear off to Philadephia, Pennsylvania!" He cut a quick glance at Link. "Bet you think that was the end of it, bartender. If so, you think wrong. Somebody . . . *somebody* took a trip all the way to Philadelphia, Pennsylvania, and murdered poor Ev Cramer right in his sister's house. Shot him to bits right there—and then, by God, strangled a little parlor maid to death

66

who happened to see the shooting." There were tears in MacDuff's eyes.

"You say I said any of this . . ." MacDuff brushed his coat sleeve across his eyes. "Ev Cramer . . . was a very decent fellow. He was . . . a particular friend of mine."

Link thought MacDuff was acting more like an Irishman than a Scot. He'd heard complaints of good men done under by gangs for most of his life. It was a way of the world. And he supposed that MacDuff was doing all this talking simply because he'd seen a Coe man, even if only a drover, beaten. That was a sad thing. And it was unusual, if true, for men to go to such lengths to punish a defaulter. It was odd, just the same, to be sitting in MacDuff's office, hearing his complaints when, in the not too distant past, he'd been one of the fellows poor MacDuff was complaining of. There'd always been some action, in gambling or in business, for a man, or a man and his friends, if they were handy with guns, didn't mind standing up to a shooting. There was always some slice of business for fellows like that. Always had been for him, anyway.

MacDuff drew a deep breath. He glanced at Link again, and looked sorry to have said so much. "So, you better step light in Colt Creek, bartender. Wilson Coe may think it's funny, you knocking that drover on his arse. But old Anse may not think it's funny at all. You see his boys come in here, you watch out!" He cleared his throat, and stood up, scraping the chair back. Link stood up, too.

"Thanks for the advice," he said. He waited to see if MacDuff had anything more to say, but the owner—the part-owner—was standing looking out the grimy window again. It was almost dark out there now. Dark, and windy, and cold.

Not that he was shying, but Link took a good look around the big room as he walked down the stairs from the balcony. He was considering the wisdom of just clearing out. It had been a busy enough day—that stable girl, and the rough-house with those men. Then, the loud-mouth drover.

Might be much the better part of valor to go and saddle the lame brown and get limping out of this town. If the Coes were the sort to carry small grudges, they might decide to make an example of an upstart bar-wiper. But Link had seen no gunmen in the town at all. No hard-cases, in the White Rose or out of it. No rowdies on the streets, no corner boys or loafers looking for a fight. Which all might mean a peaceable town, or a town with a lid clamped down firm by the Coes.

No question, though, Wisdom said: vamoose.

But it was cold and windy weather out there. All the colder and windier for a man with grey in his hair, a limping horse, and nothing in his pocket but some pilfered bar-change.

Too damn cold and too damn windy.

Link went back behind the bar. He noticed, as he poured double shots of Chicago whiskey for two cattle buyers already several sheets to the wind, that Wilson Coe no longer stood at the end of the bar. Wasn't in the saloon at all. Nothing to be made of that.

The cattle buyers were talking about the war. One of them had had a brother in the Iron Brigade. Dead and gone, of course. Dead and gone.

Link slept deep.

And dreamed deep. He dreamed he was riding trail, riding far, far out onto the prairie. Riding deep into the high grass . . .

Birds . . . grasshoppers, all rose under his horse's

hooves in small clouds. Bluebells studded the grass stems, and as he rode, he could see the grass bending in slow waves before a distant wind. The grass, like a deep, bright carpet—soft greens, pale yellows, the small, quick flashes of flower-blue—stretched away farther than he could see. Farther than he would ever see.

He was not riding the brown. He was riding an Appaloosa stud, a horse he knew. It breasted the high grass, and the stems folded back along the horse's flanks as waves do from the bow of a sailing ship.

It was the buffalo grass country.

The way it had been when he was young.

He dreamed he rode the whole morning long. He dreamed the creak and sweat of the saddle; the smell of the easy striding horse; the heat of the sun across the side of his jaw, where his hatbrim did not shade. He could smell the air. Sometimes he did think he might be dreaming, but it was a passing thought.

Then he saw a woman standing in the grass. She was standing in his way, but distant. Standing with her bonnet in her hand, the fierce sun striking glints from her hair. She was wearing black.

Someone spoke to him, but when he turned in the saddle, they were gone. When he looked ahead, though, the woman was still there, standing in the thick, wide-swayed grass, the stems, the flowers as high as her breasts. Higher, so that only her shoulders, her white throat appeared above the greens and yellows shifting in contrary winds.

He knew that woman. He now had ridden very close, and missed having ridden much of the way. It was one of the times he thought he might be dreaming . . .

She was a ranch woman. Not pretty in a nice town way, perhaps, but sweet-faced, strong, with brave eyes. She looked like a handsome mare turned human. She knew him. And called to him. She raised her hand as he rode by. She called: "Wait!" And he tried. He pulled the Appaloosa up, tried to pull him up, but the animal had the bit in his teeth, and wouldn't stop, wouldn't hold up or even slow. Link turned in the saddle, turned his head to keep the woman in sight, and hauled on the reins like a madman, cursing, swearing at the horse. But it was no good. Even in the dream, Link realized it was a magic horse, a horse that obeyed no man.

He kicked out of the stirrups, threw his leg over, and slid from the saddle into the grass, and the horse was gone.

And the woman was gone as well. Hidden from him deep in the high grass. For the grass now grew over Link's head, over his head by inches. And was growing as he watched. The horse was gone, and his journey with it. And he wouldn't find the woman again.

He woke to someone's knocking on the liquor-room door. The small room was dark; the sheepherder's stove, almost cold, ticked softly in its corner. Link felt he'd been asleep for quite a while. He yawned, and stretched like a fireside dog. The knocking came again. He heard the Negro swamper, George, say something through the door.

Link swung his bare feet to the cold rough plank floor, got up, and gathered his clothes from where he'd piled them by the stove. If they'd been warm, they weren't any more.

"Hold your horses, dammit—be right there!" George had started knocking on the door again.

Link buckled on his gun-belt, went to the door, drew the bolt, and swung it open. George was standing there, leaning on a wet mop. "Sheriff to see you,

Mister Link." He didn't seem nervous about it, so there seemed no reason for Link to be, either. He wasn't wanted for anything in this territory or in any other that he knew about, except possibly California— perhaps Old Mexico, too. Nothing around here, unless that drover last night, or the boys in the hay loft had made some complaint . . .

"You tell him I'll be right there." George nodded, and strolled away, trailing his wet mop through the sawdust. The edge of the bar cabinet cut off most of the view of the saloon's main room, and Link didn't try any careful peeping. He stepped out past the end of the bar, looking down the length of gleaming mahogany toward the bat-wing doors.

It was sunny out there, the warm yellow light flooding in through tall windows, through the slats in the swinging doors. It was late, maybe eleven o'clock. No one was in the place except George, and a stocky little man he was speaking to, delivering the message.

Link walked down the bar toward them. He had the sun in his eyes, but that didn't concern him. He'd never had the sun bother him in a fight. You just looked at the man you were after; you could generally see him, sun glare or no. Balconies, on the other hand, could be a bother. He glanced up along the length of balcony overlooking the front of the saloon. A careful lawman might had set a deputy up there with a shotgun in case of some unpleasantness.

No shotgun. No deputy.

George had wandered on his way, and the stocky man stood watching Link come toward him. He wasn't just stocky, Link saw. He was fat. A fat little old man in a big hat. A dented badge was pinned to his checkered shirt. He wore a break-top .38 for a cross draw, but Link doubted if the old fellow could have reached around his belly for the pistol in time to do

71

any good at all.

The old man reached up to tilt his hat back on his head to get a better look as Link walked up to him, but he kept the hat on. A lot of old timers had grown up keeping their hats on in public places. When he reached up like that, Link saw that the old man's fingers were swollen, knob-jointed with rheumatism.

The sheriff had the clear blue eyes many old men seemed to show. Those eyes were giving Link the look that old lawmen used on strangers. The look that said: I know damn well you've done *something*, at some time or another. But I may not care enough to dig into it. Just you go along, and mind your manners.

"You Fred Link?"

"Yes, I am. What can I do for you, Sheriff?" Town marshal would be more like it, Link thought. "Sheriff" was a courtesy title.

The little sheriff looked down at the Bisley Colt's, and then back up to Link's face. "You ever use that on a man?" he said.

"Once or twice, when I was younger, and foolish," Link said, and smiled.

The sheriff grunted, considering that. "Favor oak sticks, do you?"

So it *was* the drover, last night. Link was surprised the man had complained. Most cowpokers took barroom damage for granted. "Only when I'm forced to it to keep a customer from being abused," he said. "The drover was mistreating one of the women here. He wouldn't quit."

The sheriff grunted again, taking that in. Link could see he had once been a sturdy man, short and broad, probably a good fellow with his fists. It seemed to him, however, that the old man was not suited to his job, anymore, unless he was a Coe man, and in on a pass. Which seemed likely enough.

Wrong. "I don't blame any man for putting one of the Coe people in their place if the Coe man started it," the old man said, "but what I won't have is a trail-bum coming into this town and causing trouble to start where there was no trouble! Do you hear me, Buster?"

No doubt about it; in his day the little fellow must have been a hard-case policeman.

"I hear you, Sheriff," Link said. "I'm just here to work for enough money to move on." Ought to cool the old man off. And it seemed to. The sheriff's gaze wandered into the depths of the saloon.

"Where's MacDuff?" he said.

"I wouldn't know, Sheriff."

"Well, I don't want you being behind that bar tonight. It's Saturday,"—news to Link; he'd lost track on the trail—"and those men from the 'D' will all be in here. Charlie Coe, too, more than likely. No place for you, drifter." The clear blue eyes shifted back to Link's face.

"Oh, I'll be here, Sheriff. But I'll just slide out the beers and mind my own bee'swax." The sheriff looked for a moment as if he might dispute that, but he decided against it.

"Just see that you do," he said. "See that you do mind your own business. And don't be taking any more sticks to people, understand?"

"Sure do," Link said. "And now, if you don't mind, I've got to get my breakfast. We'll have customers in here soon."

The little sheriff grunted, turned on his heel, and walked out through the bat-wing doors. He walked with a kind of bandy-legged strut, like an old rooster, crippled up, but game. A considerable amount of cold air was coming through those bat-wing doors; Link thought he'd ask George why the winter doors had been taken down. It was too damn early in the year to

73

take them down, that was for sure. Cold as a banker's heart.

The old Chinaman was in the kitchen, rubbing blacking on the big iron range. He looked up when Link came in and stared at him for a moment. Then he went back to his blacking.

"Too late for some breakfast?"

The old man shook his head. "No. I'll cook for you. You want eggs—ham?" Link sat at the long table. George and the two fat girls were nowhere to be seen. Link figured it must have taken something special to call them away from the kitchen warmth, and the food.

"Why were the winter doors taken down out there? It's too damn cold; those pot-bellies aren't keeping up at all." Sounded like an old man himself. Something of the sort must have occurred to the old Chinaman, because he smiled as he set a big skillet down on the stove with a soft clang.

"It was warmer last week," he said. His long white beard, doubled up under his chin with a length of string, waggled when he talked. He went through the back door to the larder, a small cleaver in his hand, and, after a minute or two, came back to holding a fresh sliced ham steak an inch and some thick. "I give you this morning's biscuits," he said, and laid the ham down in the skillet with a little hiss of steam and spattering fat.

"Cold biscuits'll be fine," Link said.

The Chinaman poked at the ham with a long-handled fork. "Last night, I know who you are," he said, peering at the ham as if it might be causing trouble in the skillet.

Link went cold to the bone. He eased the kitchen chair back out of his way, and slowly stood up. Where

74

had the old man put that damn cleaver? Then he saw it in the rack behind the stove. If he shot the cook, and went out the back . . . down the side street . . . across Main . . . He'd have to steal a horse. The brown wasn't up to it. Not up to a long chase, however long a chase these people might mount for an old cook. Which might be considerable, after all; the Chinaman was a damn good cook!

"That is the look I knew," the old man said, looking sideways at Link. "Last night; I heard trouble"—he motioned toward the doorway into the saloon with his head—"I looked out there, and saw you hit that cowboy." He looked back down at the ham, and gave it a sharp little poke with the fork, making it mind its manners. "That look in your face I remember. Jao Feng! God of furious war." He flipped the ham steak over with a quick darting motion of the fork, and it hissed and spattered anew.

"What in the world are you talking about, old man?" Might be nothing to it, after all.

"I saw you shoot a man called Louis Pinchot in a poker game at Herman's Fine Beef Restaurant in El Paso in Texas," the old Chinaman said. "You shot him under the table and when he cried out, you shot him in his face." The old man gestured at the back of his head. His white pig tail there was as wispy as his beard. "All of his things came out of his head back here," he said, and chuckled, apparently with some pleasure at the memory.

Link's Colt's was in his hand. Make up your mind, gunman. Make up your mind. If the old man tells that tale to anybody else, then Fred Link becomes Buckskin Frank Leslie and a nine-day wonder, a human two headed calf for everybody to come and stare at. For kids to try and shoot at. For older men to come and shoot at, as well.

A killer long dead and gone, in most people's minds, suddenly come to life. They'd buy him beers at first, then they'd find some fool, and egg on a fight, just so they could say they'd seen it. Then, likely as not, they'd call in a Federal Marshal and his men to hunt this mad dog gunman down.

Oh, old man, old man, why couldn't you just keep quiet? Why couldn't you have hugged your secret, and kept still?

Link eared back the hammer on the Colt's.

The Chinaman looked at him and grinned—two or three teeth left in the bottom jaw, that was all he had. "Jao Feng!" he said. "Look just like that!" He chuckled, and took another glance at the ham. It seemed to be behaving properly. He touched it with the flat of the fork tines, but he didn't poke at it. "I will keep your secret, Mister Leslie," he said, and sounded like some Chinese villain in a San Francisco melodrama. "Mister Louis Pinchot was no friend of mine."

Link noticed the old man had no trouble with his 'R's. He talked like any old man who'd been around.

Link remembered Louis Pinchot very well. Pinchot'd been a cook, too. One of Herman's steak cooks. He'd been a bully boy, with a habit of looking into the discards. Link had warned him once. But Pinchot had been tough stuff, a small bright-eyed Frenchie who liked making bigger men back down. He carried a pocket pistol, and was called by some a better than fair shot with it.

Link had warned him. But Pinchot was tough stuff; he'd known who Link was, but that hadn't made him shy. He'd stared at Link as a man might at a piece of dog shit on his boot, then he'd reached out to flip through the discards with his left hand while his right eased down into his coat pocket. Link supposed he meant to fire through the coat material, if he were rushed.

Drawing a large revolver under a table while sitting in a sprung-butt chair is a trick only a young man would have practiced.

Link had been just that kind of young man, that kind of fool. Little French bully-cook had had no chance.

The first round had taken him straight through his lunch. The second, to the head, had killed him.

The old Chinaman speared the ham steak and heaved it out of the skillet and onto a battered tin plate. He sighed happily. "Louis Pinchot," he said, "salted everything."

Link put his revolver in its holster, and sat down to eat his breakfast.

CHAPTER 6

IF TROUBLE was coming in with the Rocking-D men, it didn't arrive for the midday rush. Parker, with the same murmured report on his mother—feeling a deal better, thank you, Mister Link . . . able to take vegetable soup and keep down every drop—was dead on time and up to the job as usual, as long as he didn't have to tend the whole bar. Though one man, no matter how good, would have had his hands full drawing beers and pouring drinks for that crowd. The White Rose was one of five full-fledged saloons in town, not counting barrel-houses, cribs and whore-house bars, but it seemed there was plenty of thirst to go around. Feed store clerks were a major item today. Every second man at the mahogany smelled of oats and alfalfa, and had wisps of it clinging to his coat. It reminded Link to go and check on the brown, see if the splint was down or not. Check on the girl, too.

It would be a fine thing if she'd had another fit after he'd left her. Choked on her tongue while he was paddling beers for a pack of drummers or whacking that loud-mouth drover across the head. That would be a fine thing. Take advantage of a half-wit girl, and then leave her sick and alone. A manly action, all in all. A fine thing.

Near two o'clock, the rush slackened—all the feed-store clerks back to their counters and scales, thank God. Link had forgotten how hard bartending was on the feet. It was one thing to whip up a knacky cocktail for some sport. It was another to do your rush hours running back and forth down a long bar passing beer to a herd of men who smelled and sounded enough like beeves to be in danger of getting shipped to Kansas City themselves.

High-heel boots were fine in a stirrup. They were less than handy on a pair of aching feet behind a thirty-five foot bar. Now Link knew why old bartenders used to work in their slippers. He'd once thought that was very funny, those fat old fellows flapping along behind the bar in their run-overs. Not so funny, now.

He was damned glad to see the last customer—save two or three just hanging around the wood for talk and slow service—head out the door. And damn MacDuff for not keeping the winter doors up! Stoves and all, and the crowd not withstanding, it had been chilly in the Rose all afternoon.

"I'll clean up, Mister Link."

"Damn me if I won't let you, Parker." And welcome to it.

Link went out back—the Chinaman gave him a look and a wink as he went through the kitchen—and took his ease in the Crapper, reading the overall advertisements from the Sears-Roebuck Catalog while he did so. Prices were headed higher. Fairly soon, a common working man would be walking around bare-arsed!

There were some people at the livery stable—a

79

man, his wife, and a pair of twin boys as alike as peas. They were renting a buggy to go out to some ranch, and making a great fuss about it, examining the buggy, lifting it to spin the wheels, conferring about the horses (as plain a pair of stable plugs as Link had ever seen) and generally making cakes of themselves before Patterson, the old Beanpole who owned the livery, and the girl.

She stood holding the horses' heads, dull-eyed and dreaming, scrawny in her dirty jean trousers and old blue shirt. She looked well enough—no sign of the fits or the epilepsy, or whatever it had been. Link was relieved to see that, and embarrassed to see the girl again. He thought that maybe she'd do something to show what had happened between them—let everybody in town know it, too. But she didn't. She glanced at him, where he stood by the troughs, but it was a dull, animal glance. She didn't even seem to know who he was, or remember what had happened.

When the buggy-renter, a handsome man in a black broadcloth suit, finally professed himself satisfied and handed his family up, Patterson came stilting over to Link, accepted another week's hay-and-board from him—MacDuff's cash-drawer had suffered in the noon rush—and shouted to the girl to take him back and show him the brown's leg.

She had to wait while the handsome man in broadcloth settled himself and gathered the reins, carefully clucked to the plugs, and signaled her to let go their heads. He was apparently expecting quite a spirited dash out of the stable yard. The plugs sighed, farted, and led out at a slow walk. Still, the fellow had them well up to their bits, and the admiration of his family with it.

During this, Patterson talked to Link about the war, and asked, with some roundaboutation, what unit of the Confederacy he'd fought in. It was a question Link was used to, and he modestly lied about some heroic service as a boy cavalryman. Patterson seemed satisfied with this, nodding as if it was just what he'd expected, and made some cutting remarks about grasping Yankee bankers.

The girl came over, and stood waiting until her uncle was finished talking. Then she led Link back into the stable, through it, across a little yard with a grain safe and a pump in it, and on to a stall-shed, that, from the sounds beyond it, bordered the lumber yard. Link could see why he needed a guide this time to find the brown. They'd—or the girl had—put him into a close stall, and wrapped a hot posset of mash around the cannon. The burlap was tied up as neatly as in a racing stable. The girl's work, for sure.

She knelt beside the brown, and pressed the poultice, to show Link the leg wasn't hurting the animal anymore. Nothing stupid about the girl then. There was some light in her eyes as well. Probably felt safer with animals than people. Avoided people, more than likely, until her heat came on her.

"That's good work," Link said to her. "That's very good!" He nodded to make sure she understood him. It was hard to tell. He thought of giving her some of poor MacDuff's change, but it was likely the Beanpole took care to get that from her. Link thought a minute, then reached into his back pocket and pulled out his bandanna—fresh washed yesterday, and a pretty piece of cloth, yellow, with a fine pattern on it in red. She eyed it, and he saw she liked the color.

When he held it out to her, she seemed upset at first, and shook her head, but Link took one of her work-hardened little hands, put the handkerchief in it, and closed her fingers over the cloth.

"It's for you," he said, and nodded to the doctoring

on the brown's leg. "For doing such a fancy job of it."

Then she took the bandanna, and put it down her shirt. She seemed pleased. It was hard to tell. As for the brown, well, he was a plug and no mistake a mistake about it; but cured up, he might do to ridge out of town. Link had been figuring him as a dead loss. Worth a bandanna to get him rideable again. And for sure the girl needed some joy of a pretty.

Link left the livery, and walked out on the town. The long sleep, the rich breakfast, had left him rested, feeling very well, and glad for the crisp air and bright sunshine of this mountain country.

He strolled the town's high boardwalks, considering the purchase of a new jacket. Buckskin, for sure. It didn't have the warmth of wool, but there was a style to it. A reminder, as well, of too many years to throw away. The best, of course, would be Crow indian made; those women knew how to work buckskin. Tanned it with brains and piss and whatnot, kept it soft and supple after any rain that might come down. Of course, it would have to wait; even an inferior article would have to wait. There was a limit to the damage MacDuff's cash-drawer could sustain. Already been bitten pretty deep.

Would be time, in a week or so, to try a little penny-ante poker with those feed store clerks. They seemed a fine bunch of young men. Very ripe for higher education.

Colt Creek appealed to Link as he patrolled the town, window-shopping in hardwares, dry goods, one haberdashery, two gunsmiths, four restaurants—each looking worse than the one previous. At the edge of town, after a hike through pasture and cold, stiff mud, he looked out a small church of no particular denomination, and, across another pasture, a small two-storey house, painted light blue, that boasted a suspicious amount of fresh laundry, much of it feminine, flapping on lines in its back yard amongst the chickens. Link wasn't even tempted, a circumstance he ascribed to that rut with the stable girl, and, may as well admit it, his age.

It didn't trouble him. He was in better spirits than he'd known for some time. A job, a warm bed, some of MacDuff's small change in his pockets. All were to the good.

It occurred to Link that some of the Coe people might come in after all, to make some trouble for him. Seemed unlikely, but he'd long ago learned that people did the damndest things, and it was well to keep in mind that they did. He felt he might spare a few rounds for some revolver practice, if he could find a place lonesome enough. Taking a wide circle back in the general direction of town, he came across more pasture—next day he might walk out the other way, take a look at the stock yards, see if those men were ever sober—then ran into a field of brambles. Blackberries, likely, in the summer, now only whips of thorns to take the hide off a man. He stomped on through. Odd how a man's feet would hurt at his work, and feel fine tramping.

Past the briars was a good place for him. A small wash, already starting to fill with swift brown run-off from the mountains to the west. Not a foot deep yet, though. The curving length of the bank would do for him—nothing but packed mud and tree roots, a clear field for fire. He looked around before he climbed down the bank; nobody in sight, horse or foot.

Cartridges cost money. A few shots, either hand . . .

He drew while he was still awkward, stepping sliding down the steep mud, drew and shot at a bent brown root a little over twenty-five feet away. The root was at a hard angle to his right.

83

Clean miss by maybe three, four inches. He holstered the Bisley, hit the creek-bottom flats hard with both boots and drew and fired again, the root almost behind him then, and over thirty feet away.

Miss. Maybe an inch to the left.

Link put the revolver away, and stood thinking about his shooting, kicking idly at a buried white stone with the toe of his left boot. He wasn't concerned about missing. Those had been two difficult shots; in a fight, he would have fired again at once, and hit with the second shot. What troubled him slightly was his pulling to the left, with the pressure of his hand on the grip, at the second shot. It wasn't poor pressure on the trigger. The Bisley's trigger didn't allow for any serious pressure before it set the piece off.

He finally decided that it was simply lack of practice, not a bad fault in his grip on the weapon. He turned the other way, upstream, and turned back, drew, and fired at the root again. He missed it to the right by a hair, but was no longer concerned. He'd tried to compensate, and hadn't needed to; his grip had settled in.

He put the revolver up, drew again, and shot the root in two. Then he put the revolver in its holster, drew, and broke a small stone across the stream. He felt that was about enough for the right hand, drew once more, and clipped a branch from a broke-trunk larch a good way down the wash.

Then he reloaded, tossed the Colt's into his left hand and tried some fast, steady shooting. That went very well.

Link came out of the wash near the trail he'd ridden coming into town, and he hiked along that at a good swinging pace, enjoying the scenery. It had been a considerable walk, and about now he wouldn't have minded having a good horse under him. But it was a pleasant weariness. He could see what those Boston people got out of their walks. You saw more, somehow, walking rather than jogging along on a horse like a mailed package. The pleasant odor of gunsmoke clung about him, mingling with the fresh mountain air.

It occurred to him that the brown's leg was healing fast and that, on the off chance the Coes might take the beating of their drover unkindly, a quiet exit from Colt Creek might be advisable in the next day or two.

He would think about it. Target practice was one thing. A fight was something else. The last few years, any fight with guns had cost him more than he'd won. Keep his head down tonight, for sure, and think about it . . .

He thought he felt something in the ground under his feet and at the same moment heard the distant thud and mutter of hoofbeats, the faint jingle of harness chain. A team of some kind, coming fast.

He stopped and turned back to see what was coming. It was a stagecoach, rolling fast down the long easy slope into Colt Creek. The driver was pushing his horses. Much more of a slope, and the Concord would free-wheel, and maybe run the horses down. He could see the driver's whip curling up over his head, heard the "pop" of the lash.

Link didn't see quite enough room on the trail for him and the coach both. He stepped over to the side and down into a shallow ditch the town had likely dug for run-off water.

The coach was coming mighty fast, bouncing and swaying, pitching hard over the road ruts as it came. The chests of the leaders were dark with sweat under their harness; their hooves kicked up clods as they galloped. Link saw that the coachman looked damn young to be springing a stage that way; the shotgun was a withered customer with an eye-patch, looked to be having trouble holding on, the way the vehicle was jouncing. Link could hear the passengers yelling. Hard to tell if they were enjoying themselves or were scared to death.

Then it was up to him going like hell. And while he stood staring like a hayseed hick, the driver's lash licked out and down quicker than a snake and snapped Link's hat clean off his head.

"Get a horse, Sport!" the boy-coachman's snotty voice.

Link's old Stetson was scaling away like a pie plate and the Concord was past and gone in a shower of mud which spattered Link toes to nose.

So much for this fucking Boston walking! Link stood in the ditch as mad as fire. Done like the greenest horn on the hill, by God! And having the pleasure of hearing the passengers laugh as they rolled away. Like had never before seen the sense of stagecoach robbing. Now, it was seeming more reasonable.

He watched the coach out of sight down the slope and on into Main Street, and then he went looking for his hat. He found the Stetson under a bush. The whiplash had nicked the brim. Damn little snot could have taken out an eye! Well, suppose it served him right for walking in riding country; bound to look a fool. The humor of it began to strike Link. Buckskin Frank Leslie out for a stroll—has his hat lifted like any rube's. Leaves the great man furious . . .

Still, it would be a pleasure to confront that coaching pup. Perhaps teach him some manners. A dunk in a horse trough would be about right.

Link put on his notch-brim hat, and walked into town.

He had no trouble spotting the coach. The big stage was drawn up outside a small livery stable on Main, the passengers all unloaded, the last of the mail sacks being handed down to the livery man. A halfbreed looking fellow, who appeared to run the U.S. Postal Service in Colt Creek as well. It was the shotgun doing the hand-downing toothless, with a patch. The driver was nowhere to be seen.

Link's temper came back to him, just a mite, when Toothless, perched on top of the stage, saw him in the street and apparently recognized him, for he gave out a flap-lipped guffaw.

"Weel! Hidy thar! See you done hunted down yore hat!" and more of the same. Link strolled up to the Concord, grinning like a fool pleased enough to have the joke on him. "Right neat whip-work, wun't you say?" said Toothless. "That plum is a pisser, shore 'nuff!" He switched ends, up to the coach roof, and called down to other side. "Say, Plum! That chucklehead's here to say howdy!" Link supposed the driver had just come out of the livery to hear this piece of raillery.

He turned in his tracks while the guard was still shouting his jokes to the other side, ducked around the end of the coach and saw the kid driver standing up on the boardwalk with his hands on his hips, looking up at the guard. His back was to Link.

Here's a surprise for you, sonny! Link went up the boardwalk steps in a rush, caught the man around the waist, heaved him off his feet, and dumped him off the edge of the walk and into a full horse trough four feet below.

It wasn't until the boy had rolled out of his arms with a screech of rage, that Link realized he'd felt tits—and mighty healthy ones at that—under the driver's sheep-skin.

The girl hit the dirty water with a mighty splash, flailed out, and sank.

"Jumpin' Jesus God Almighty," Toothless said from the top of the coach. The Postal Service man stood staring, his mouth open like a fresh-caught trout's.

For the life of him, Link couldn't think of a damn thing to say. He heard the girl below him struggling up out of the scum-slippery trough.

Finally, he leaned out and looked down, just as she heaved herself over the trough edge, slipped, and rolled full length in the mud of the street.

"I'm sorry about this, ma'am—I didn't know you were a woman."

It wasn't a helpful thing to say.

That girl knew some words he'd never heard. He wasn't even sure what some of them meant, but the round, freckled face glaring up at him (she'd just put a water-melted derby hat back on her head? was as full of murder as he'd ever seen, so it seemed to Link that a stroll, or even something faster, away from there would be a mighty good idea. While it wouldn't be true to say that he just ran off, then and there, it was true that he strolled away without any unnecessary delay. In some haste, it could be said.

He reached the White Rose without the girl or a lynch mob catching up to him. She was probably too busy wringing out, and he supposed the townspeople would think a woman who dressed like a man could be expected to take a man's chances, and not complain at the result. At least, that was what Link hoped they'd think. Even in a barb like Colt Creek, a man could get a hemp necktie for roughing a woman. Even a whore, sometimes.

He ducked under the bar-trap with a sigh of relief. Parker was there already, polishing glasses—a waste of time, if ever there was one, for the sort of customers the Rose got.

"Is anything the matter, Mister Link?"

"Not a damn thing. I hope you don't call that glass clean?!"

It seemed the fair Amazon hadn't tracked him down as she appeared likely to want to do. Well into the evening, Link kept an eye peeled to the batwing doors, expecting to see the lady driver come storming in with her whip or worse, and dressed as anything from a street Dolly to a cavalry trooper. He'd met a number of odd-dressed ladies through the years, Jane Canary and others, and most of them had been tough as hickory knots. A woman who threw away the advantage of her skirts—a sensible woman, not a little half-wit like the stable girl—had to be hard-cased, out here, to see it through. Ex-whores, most of them, lady-lovers, some. Women who found rousting and rounding with cow-pokers, gamblers, pimps and sports more to their taste than sewing bees, whether in parlor houses or house parlors. The girl coachman had at least looked fair enough. Most free women looked pretty rough.

He was making a brandy sour for a show-off buyer from Chicago, using bottled lime juice more suited for a British man o' war than a cocktail, when it occurred to Link that he had done, in the two days he'd been in town, a fair amount of enemy-collecting. The loafers in the hayloft (hadn't seen hide nor hair of that bunch! must drink at another ken), that nasty drover he'd beaned, and now, the coaching Amazon. He poured the show-off his brandy sour, reflecting that the longer he stayed in Colt Creek, the more likely it was one of those chickens would be coming home to roost.

The beef buyer flourished his cocktail, swigged it down, and pronounced to his friends at the wood that it was "damn near like a Palmer House drink."

Link smiled some thanks at the man, and caught a ten cent tip.

It was a Saturday evening, right enough. And it brought back memories for Link. Memories of a lot of Saturday nights, when he stood in front of the bar, not behind it, and wore a fine bespoke San Francisco suit made of English serge, and silk smalls and a white silk shirt all fresh back from cleaning in China, by God, aboard a Craven Company clipper. Fine cheroots, sapphire studs, French cognac—the real McCoy, not this Spanish stuff—and women from the Opera House ballet. Plump girls, good girls, who only bedded for love. Or maybe for kind attention and fine jewelry. But nice girls; not whores. Girls with white shoulders and little hands as soft as babies.

Cigar smoke, and French perfume, and the click of poker chips on a green baize table . . .

Only a few years of that. But those kind of years mark a man. Score him with pleasure so that other pleasures seem limited and rough.

There were pleasures in traveling the mountain country, of course, or had been, once. And the grasslands were beautiful to ride, or had been, before the big winter and all the fences that came in then.

Still, if one of those plump, white-shouldered girls from the Follies or the Opera Ballet had taken his hand, at a party, say, and turned it over, and pretended to read his future for him in his palm, and said, "In ten years, or fifteen, you'll have grey in your hair, Frank, and you'll be all alone. You'll be tending bar in a little town in the middle of God knows where. You'll be broke, and stealing from the owner's cash drawer for a stake." If one of them had said this to him, Frank Leslie would have put back his handsome head and laughed long and loud. That wouldn't have been his notion of his future at all.

Not at all.

Link paddled the foam from two beers and skated them down the bar to two leathery old ranchers—small-holders, from the frayed cuffs of their shirts. Then he trailed on down the duck-boards to collect the owed from the drinking line.

CHAPTER 7

As THE night wore on, Link decided the lady driver had not been able to track him down—just another stranger, after all, in a crowded Saturday cow-town. If she didn't happen to frequent saloons, or at least not this saloon, he figured he was safe from a tongue-lashing, if not worse.

The Rose was full and rumbling. The pack of customers made it warm, at least. The air was a haze of cigar smoke, and thick with the wood smoke smell of outdoorsmen's bodies, the odor of red-hot cast iron from the pot-bellies. And a torrent of noise, men talking, boasting, arguing, braying with laughter at some tomfoolery. No question about it, there was something about the White Rose. It damn sure wasn't the free lunch, and likely not the beer or whiskey, either. And the place carried no girls, barring the two fat deaf-and-dumb sisters. Still, MacDuff got his customers in. Likely it was a friendly air to the ken that brought them in. Some saloons were bad bars through and through, with fights and killings common, and some ran fast games, rigged and run to pull the suckers. But the Rose appeared to offer nothing but a big, easy, companionable place for a tired workman to come and drink and talk at the top of his voice with his friends.

Link had noticed before, that many men on the frontier, or what used to be the frontier, found it to be a rougher place than they really liked, and, though driven to act the parts expected of them, found considerable relief in not having to do that.

The White Rose seemed to be a peaceful place of that sort. Relatively peaceful, at any rate.

He signaled to Parker that he was going out back to the necessary, ducked under the bar-trap, worked his way through the crowd, and went out through the side corridor to the kitchen. He got another notion of the Rose's prosperity there. The old Chinaman was cooking for some men crowded around the long kitchen table. Platters of deep fried chicken, and steaks fried in the same fat, and soup bowls full of smoking hot canned peach cobbler. The men were yelling to each other just as loudly as in the main room in front, but the noise was somewhat muffled by their mouths being full of food. A Mason jar in the center of the table was stuffed with greenback dollars and two-bit pieces, so the customers were paying handsomely for all they could eat. Link saw a huge bearded fellow in fancy flowered suspenders that looked, from the pile of chicken and t-bones on his platter, to be starting in on his third or fourth full dinner. A mixing bowl full of steaming cobbler stood at his elbow, waiting its turn.

The old Chinaman winked at Link as he went through the crowd to the back door, and out into the cool, clear night air. He might be mistaken, but it seemed to Link that the air no longer had a wintry bite to it. Perhaps Spring had come to the high country to stay. It would be a relief. There was more than enough moon to pick his way through the piles of cut wood and assorted trash and broken furniture and stacked lumber, brick-piles, and what-not, apparently for some future addition to the Rose MacDuff had planned.

There was a line at the out-house for crapping—common piss-ants were scattered through the big yard in moonlight, peeing in beer drinkers' happy fashion. Link walked out to a clump of brush a good ways off, unbottoned his flies, and joined the others in that gentle easing. Peeing by moonlight . . . watching the thin golden stream arching away into the shrubbery. What a great number of men must have stood, pissing by moonlight, thinking their thoughts.

He shook his dick, tucked in, buttoned up, and walked back into the Rose. The Chinaman, busy at his stove, winked at him again. And he noticed the huge man had started on his bowl of cobbler. Looked good, at that. Might come in and make a supper himself in a while.

He noticed the difference at once.

The big room was quieter, for one thing. And there wasn't so much laughing. Men were talking softer, keeping their attention to themselves and their friends nearby. Men had their heads down.

Link looked for the cause, and saw it.

The red-faced drover had come into the place, and was sitting, talking to two other men at a center table between the two stoves. The drover was talking loud, japing, his voice odd past his broken nose. The nose was a blue-bruised knot, and the right side of his face was mottled black and yellow with bruising. Link wondered that he felt like coming out drinking, with a painful face like that. Likely it wasn't his idea.

The two men with him were the cause of quiet at MacDuff's saloon.

One, a man in his thirties, was a shaggy-haired

94

fellow with a long preacher's nose and pleasant brown eyes. He was dressed in a cheap grey suit that buttoned up high, and the side of the suit-coat was hiked up over a holstered Smith and Wesson Russian Model revolver. He was sitting back in his chair in an easy, relaxed sort of way. He had a glass of beer in his left hand, resting on the table. He wasn't drinking it.

Link had seen the other man before. A boy, really. It was the fat boy who had galloped past him in the street the day before, the one who'd called, "Hey, Dad. You better trot!" He was wearing a green shirt now, not the red spotted one. But he still wore the two parrot-grip .38's: Colt's. The gunbelt was tucked under the roll of belly-fat spilling over his pants waist. He couldn't have been more than seventeen, eighteen years old.

He had a pig's face—alert, round, intelligent, fat, and dangerous. He had pig's eyes, as well—bulging, pale, lashless blue.

Link wondered how the hell he had missed the boy for bad when he'd seen him riding in the street. He hadn't used to be so slow.

One of the Coe people, he supposed. None of the three were looking toward him, toward the bar. It wasn't a good sign, that careful inattention.

"Parker," Link said, when the boy came down the bar for bitters, "Who are the two with the drover?" Parker didn't ask which two he meant.

He bent his head as he poured the drops of bitters, and he kept his voice low, as if those men could hear him. "That's Charlie Coe. And the other one's Ikey Stern."

Link took the bottle out of his hand; Parker was ruining that drink. "Coe's the boy?" Parker nodded. "He's the kid brother. Billy and Reed are older . . ."

Link thought about it for a moment, catching hold

of Parker's shirt sleeve to keep him from moving away; Parker certainly seemed inclined to move away. "And the other man?"

"I told you," Parker said, trying to tug his arm loose. "Ikey Stern. He's a Jew." Link had found that most Jews thought gunmen no better than any street thugs and it was hard to argue they were wrong. There were exceptions, Jimmy Ringgold being one. Ringo, some people called him, but not to his face.

He let go of Parker's sleeve, and the boy drifted down the bar in some haste; then Link glanced up and saw that the gunman, Stern, was watching him. Their eyes met, and Stern's were intelligent and amused.

So it was trouble and no mere chance that had brought the loud drover, busted nose and all, back to MacDuff's. Someone of that bunch had decided that they couldn't have a beer-server beating up on their men. He looked into Stern's eyes as he had looked into so many similar. That knowing, rueful look their sort of men exchanged before trouble. "*Well, friend,*" that look said, "*Here we are, and here it goes. And it's probably damned foolishness.*"

Link saw that Stern realized he was, or had been, something else than a bartender. It was interesting he wasn't bothering to talk to the boy about it. Link thought it likely the boy was a poor listener.

And now he had a fast decision to make. Those two would likely have to start trouble, force him into it. Running a tough town required some attention to appearances. There was a limit to the amount of cold-blooded murder that a town full of armed men—decent fellows, most of them—would tolerate from anybody.

They'd have to force him to it, one way or another.

He could head on out the back, take the chance they hadn't covered that, cut down to the stables, get the brown, or any other horse he had to take if the brown couldn't run yet, and clear the hell out of this town, out of the country around it, as well.

There was a time he wouldn't have even thought about it. Was a time he'd have already been over at their table, pushing them, smiling, calling them out right there.

Was a time.

Link dropped the bar rag into the sink, shook his head at a customer ordering a double shot, and walked down to the bar-trap. Under the trap, down the corridor, and out.

Just as he started to duck from the trap, he saw the sheriff walk in through the batwings. The old man was strutting his tired, bandy-legged walk. As Link hesitated, he saw the old lawman's flick of a glance to him, and a longer, steadier stare toward the center table.

Couldn't be better. When the old man walked over to Coe and the other two, Link ducked under the trap and began to shoulder his way through the crowd to the corridor. Behind him, he heard a voice raised in anger. Sounded like the fat boy. Then he heard a man shout and some others.

Link turned, stepped to the side to see past a big man with a red beard, and saw that the Coe boy, grinning, was punching the old sheriff, hitting him hard in the face. "Bother who?" he was yelling. "Bother some yellow-belly bartender?" The sheriff was trying to fight back, punching out as well as he could; the old man didn't even try for his gun. "You'll mind your own damn business, I guess, you old jackass!" the boy was yelling. And he beat the old man with his fists until Link saw the sheriff's knees buckle.

Men were shouting to stop it, and two big workmen from the yard started toward the fat boy. Then Link heard Stern say, "No." He didn't say it loudly, and he had not drawn his revolver. He stood a little way from where the old man was being beaten, and pointed at those two men and said, "No." And that word stuck. The yard men stood still as elk that have heard a dangerous sound.

It didn't make sense to Link that the old sheriff would have gotten himself into such trouble over a nosy-parker bartender, particularly a man who was just passing through the town. But he had.

Get moving, you fool. You won't get another chance to duck out.

The old man was down now, and Charlie Coe, grinning, was nudging the sheriff with his boot. "He's had enough, Charlie," Stern said to him.

"You think so?" Coe said. "I think this old sack of shit has more coming!" And he bent down, gripped the sheriff's gunbelt with one hand, and his jacket collar with the other, picked the unconscious old man halfway up and hauled him to one of the cherry red stoves rumbling nearby. He pressed the old man's head against the iron.

The men in the saloon shouted, and some of them started toward Coe. But—*you fool!*—Link was faster.

He shoved the red-bearded man aside and stepped forward. Stern was good. He hadn't forgotten him. From halfway across the room he saw Link step out. He saw his face, and he went for his gun.

Stern had what Ben Thompson used to call a "hard" draw. He hit the butt of the big Smith and Wesson hard with the palm of his hand, slapping the piece up out of the holster. He was quick. It wasn't a smooth draw, but it was a quick one. He stepped to the side as he did it.

Link drew and shot him through the chest. A long shot, at least thirty feet—long for bar-room shooting,

98

anyway. But he didn't kill him; Stern's side-step placed the hit to the right of his heart.

The slug spun him, and knocked him back into some chairs and down. The Smith and Wesson went off as he fell.

Charlie Coe had looked up from the old sheriff as the shooting started, and Link saw him for an instant among an avalanche of shouting men trying to get out of the line of fire to the right and left. The men were yelling, ducking, some falling to the floor—and Link saw Coe again. He had his .38's in his hands; he'd drawn both guns. His round pig's face was swollen with rage. He was coming straight at Link in a swift waddling run and firing as he came.

Link shot him in the belly. He saw the green shirt snap just where the round went in. The fat boy was staggered, but he kept triggering the .38's. Link felt a sudden stab of ice clear through the meat of his left shoulder, and he shot the boy again, in the belly. Coe staggered back, dropping one revolver, the other still wildly firing. He was still trying to kill Link; Link could hear the bullets snapping and twanging just over his head. He almost fired into Coe a third time, but the fat boy suddenly tripped, staggering backward, and fell on the seat of his pants, still holding one of his revolvers. Then he rolled slowly onto his back, and lay still, staring at the ceiling.

The powdersmoke was thick as the devil; Link took two paces sidewards toward the bar, to clear it. He knew the boy had hit him in the shoulder. But he felt fine, even with the wound. He felt very good.

He had just begun to hear again, after the ear-splitting noise of the guns. He could hear the people shouting in the place; some people were shouting, but most of the ones he could see were crouched down or sitting frozen in their chairs, quiet.

He took another step to the end of the bar, and looked through the smoke to be sure that Stern was still down.

Suddenly, something struck him a terrible blow to his left side. It had all the terrific weighty smack of a horse's kick. The force of it shoved him hard against the bar, and he looked across the room and saw Stern up and on his feet and sighting the 44. for a second shot.

Link ducked to the left, half doubled over. His left side felt turned to wood. He couldn't feel his left foot when he stepped that way. Across the room, Stern's face looked intent and calm through the drifting fog of powdersmoke. Link could see blood running from the man's chest, soaking the front of the grey suit, turning the material black in the lamplight.

"Oh, my God," a man said.

Link and Stern fired together. Link thought he'd missed. He felt Stern's bullet thump past his ear. One of the men at the bar suddenly broke and ran past Link, right across in front of him. A plump man in a plug hat—some drummer or other. Stern hesitated a moment after the man had cleared their field of fire.

Link didn't. He center shot-Stern, and Stern fell onto his knees in the sawdust. Link tried stepping left again, to clear his smoke and finish the man, but his dead left side went wrong; he couldn't feel what he was doing and he tripped and fell over like a cut tree. He twisted in the air, trying to save himself, and his right elbow slammed down onto the bar-rail as he hit the floor. The Bisley Colt's fell loose from his hand.

It had never happened to him before, in a fight. Gun, knife, or simple stick, Link had never dropped a weapon, never fumbled a revolver in a fight. He reached for the piece, his hand scrabbling through the dirty sawdust, damp with spittle and spilled beer. And he found it—felt the curved butt with his finger tips, and gathered the gun into his grip.

He glanced across the room and froze like a rabbit with a weasel at his throat. Stern was still on his knees, propping himself off the floor with one blood-soaked arm. In his other hand, the big Smith and Wesson rested rock steady, and its muzzle, round, bottomless, and black as the devil's eye, was leveled at Link's head.

The bastard's going to kill me . . . His elbow numb, Link desperately brought the Bisley up and around, and fired. It was a miss, and he knew it.

He waited for Stern to finish everything.

Stern knelt across the room in a widening pool of blood, his eyes as calm as death down the barrel of the .44. It was very quiet in the White Rose. There wasn't a single sound.

Then, very slowly . . . very slowly, the revolver still extended, Stern leaned forward, bending down toward the floor. Bending until the muzzle of the .44 just touched the planks. Then it went off with a blast and cloud of sawdust.

Stern toppled forward into the haze of gunsmoke, and stretched out shaking, and died.

Ike Stern had run out of blood.

Link lay along the bar for a few moments. Men were beginning to murmur, say things. People werewe starting to move. Link wondered how bad the wound in his left side was. It had felt very bad. He was wondering why he felt disappointed. He hadn't wanted Stern to kill him. He certainly hadn't wanted that . . .

"Damn you people!" A man with a beard was looking down at him. "Damn you, I said—and I mean every word!" He looked down at Link, and then pointed over the bar. "Get up off the floor, and see what you've done!" He glared down at Link, mad as fire.

Link felt like laughing. Light-headed from the shooting, more than likely. He rolled over onto his stomach, and, feeling like a fool with everyone watching him, he climbed to his feet. It took him two tries to get his right leg under him so that he could get up. He couldn't feel his left leg at all. The man with the beard watched him all that time, and didn't offer him a hand.

When Link was up, holding on to the mahogany, the man pointed over the bar. Link looked, and saw young Parker sitting up on the duck-boards back there. A man who looked like a sodbuster was there with him, holding his hand. Parker was pale as a fresh washed sheet. He looked dead, already, but he was whispering to the farmer who was holding his hand.

The farmer looked up, and said to everybody, "Can we get this boy's mother here? The boy's asking for his mother!"

"If she isn't here now," Link said to the man with the beard, "she'll be too late." And he leaned over the bar. "Sorry, Parker. I'm sorry."

Parker was too far gone to hear him. Link knew now why Stern had hesitated after the panicked drummer had run between them. He must have seen his previous shot strike Parker, behind the bar. Something more to do. What in hell's fire was it?

Link looked around the room. Some men looked back at him, but most of them lowered their eyes. Not the same guts the bearded man had. He saw MacDuff looking down from the balcony, as white in the face as poor Parker.

Then he saw the red-faced drover. He was standing by some tables, looing down at Charlie Coe. Link was sick and tired of the fellow. He'd caused too damn much trouble.

Link pushed himself away from the bar and found that he could balance on his right leg and the left one, if he didn't mind no feeling in that leg, and moved carefully. A skinny boy with teeth that stuck out like a rabbit's was standing a few feet away, staring goggle-eyed at where Stern lay dead. He had an old Remington-conversion in a deep range holster dragging down his belt.

Link stepped and dragged himself over to the boy, a stable-shoveler at some ranch, by the look of him, and said, "Let me borrow this." While the boy started and then stared at him the same way he had been staring at Stern dead across the room, Link reached down, gripped the handle of the Remington, and pulled the gun out of its holster. The boy smelled pretty rank. Probably hadn't had a proper bath since he'd run away from some hard-scrabble and his Ma.

"You! Drover!" Link called. The red-faced drover turned and looked at him. Several other drovers had, too, but Red-face knew it was he that he wanted. He turned, and held both his hands up, palms out—the fingers of the right one bandages—and made a face of regret and shook his head. "By God, I swear I had no idea it would come to such a tragic pass as this!" he seemed to be saying.

Link had had enough of him. He cocked the Remington, and aimed at the fellow.

"No! No!" Someone was shouting it. Link heard some of the men calling. Odd, despairing calls. They'd thought everything was over. He saw them staring at him. Link had always liked Remingtons. Too rough for fine work, he felt. But very sturdy, honest weapons.

And so this clumsy old Conversion .44 proved. It

had a trigger-pull like a sailor's haul. But it went off.

The drover, full of regrets, was thrown back and over like a Court card turned on a table. Link heard the shot's echo, saw the soles of the fellow's boots, and heard his back strike the floor, flat, weighty, and dead as any side of beef. The people in the Rose shouted and cursed, but they stayed still. Perhaps some of them thought their bartender had gone mad.

Link walked over to look at the drover and at Coe. It was a hard walk; once he staggered and almost fell. People got out of his way. There were three men down over there. The drover was dead; Coe was lying still, staring up at the ceiling, holding his stomach with his hands. A small wet pink loop of gut was sticking up out of holes in his shirt. He was breathing, but not much.

The little sheriff lay by the stove, curled on his side. There was a charred place at the side of his head, where Charlie Coe had held him against the stove. He smelled of burning hair.

"Stop him," somebody said, in a quiet way. But there was nothing else to stop.

In a minute or so, MacDuff, still white in the face, came down and pushed his way through the crowd, and he helped Link up the stairs. When he got to the stairs, Link didn't see how he could climb them. One of the fat girls came and helped him on his other side. She was a strong girl, and he was grateful for her help. He hadn't seen how he was going to do those stairs, and that was the truth. He was feeling sick as a horse. Tired, too.

CHAPTER 8

HE WAS awake when the fat girl put him to bed in an upstairs room. He didn't know why he couldn't have his bed in the liquor room, with the sheepherder's stove. He was cold for a long time.

When he was asleep, he dreamed a doctor came in—a very young man, a kid, really, with a fuzzy blond beard. Even in the dream, this doctor hurt the hell out of him. Dug into his side, and fooled with it, and hurt the hell out of him. It was a nightmare, more than an ordinary dream. Bloody towels in it.

He woke at midday, and lay watching the sunshine outside the windows. One of the fat girls was sleeping in a chair. Link felt bandages around his chest, and a bandage that hurt him a lot more on his left shoulder. He tugged at that a little to try and make it more comfortable, but just that much trying made him feel sick to his stomach, and he was glad to get back to sleep.

When he woke again, it was morning. Sure as hell a day or two after the shooting. At least two days, he thought. He felt better, better enough to look at his right bedside for the Bisley Colt's. He had no notion that the Coes would let the matter drop with the shooting in the White Rose. He didn't think Charlie Coe had looked to be staying alive. That would make it a family matter.

"I've got it for you, if you want it." MacDuff was sitting on the other side of the bed in a straight-back chair, with a bowl of soup in his lap. He looked tired.

"Hang it off the post," Link said, "where I can reach it." His voice was cracked as an old woman's.

MacDuff bent down and put the soup on the floor, then he got up and went to a little dresser under the window, got Link's holstered revolver out of a drawer, and walked back to loop the gunbelt over the right side of the headboard where Link could reach it. Link reached up, and with some trouble, got the Colt's free —he was weak as ditch-water—and swung the gate. It was loaded.

It was hard to put it back, but he did it. Then he lay back in the pillows, getting his breath. "A baby," MacDuff said, sitting down again and picking the soup bowl up from the floor, "could waltz in here and cut your throat." He dipped a spoonful of soup and fed it to Link.

Link took all the bowl of soup. Then MacDuff handed him a red checked table napkin to wipe his mouth with. "Good service," Link said.

"Well," MacDuff said, "I suppose you've done us a favor . . ." He sighed. "At least until Bill Coe and Reed come back from Boise."

Link was feeling tired. "If the sheriff had stayed out of it, it might have come to nothing much. It was me they were after."

"Like hell they were," MacDuff said. "They didn't give a damn for you, my friend. It was the sheriff they were after." He cleared his throat. "Got him, too. That old man will never be good for anything anymore."

Link felt his face flush. Why indeed should two prime guns come hunting a bartender who'd roughed a drover? They'd had no notion of who the hell he was. Of course—it had all been play-acting, to lure the old law officer in to keep the peace! The beating had been no spur-of-the-moment thing. They'd planned to beat him, cripple him, and stop short of a badge-killling that might have brought a Federal marshal down on them. Mister Big-time Frank Leslie had simply been the small-time bait, a bartender who'd gotten too big for his britches.

"You surprised 'em," MacDuff said. "I will say that. You surprised the hell out of 'em!" He stood up, holding the empty soup bowl. "Where in the world did you learn to shoot like that?"

"In the cavalry," Link said, and MacDuff laughed. "The cavalry, huh? The whore-house cavalry, is more like it!" He stopped at the door. "There's a lady downstairs to see you. You have to use the pot?"

"No," Link said. "Who is it?" But MacDuff was already out the door.

The woman who came in the door a few minutes later, had a face like a sparrow-hawk—small, beaky, and fierce. She was dressed like a lady, and her hair was grey. She looked very much as she had nineteen years earlier in Fort Arthur, Texas.

But even if her face had changed, Link would have likely known her by her walk. She stalked into the room precisely as a bird, a hen, say, or a pigeon would have, her beaky head nodding with every stride. The sports and macks of Fort Arthur's gay life had called her Mother Carrie, making fun of that bird-walk she had, and the "chickens" she gathered. Mother Carrie Carew had been the finest cadet scout in Texas, bar none. Her stand had been at the depot usually, where she'd meet country girls coming in to see the town, and chat them, and con them, and lure them on, until the bits were safe in her boarding house. Then the captains would come and party, and break the girls in.

A smart female—and had known him well. She might not know him now, what with the scar, and the grey in his hair. Not right away, perhaps. But there'd be no fooling old Mother Carrie for long. And what the hell she was doing in Colt Creek, and why come hunting him . . .?

"Well, Jesus Christ," he said. "If it isn't Charmian Carew!"

The old terror stopped as if she were shot and stared pop-eyed at Link sitting up against his pillows. All the color had drained from her face.

"Who . . . who . . .?" Her beaky head bobbed, turned to the side, and she peered at Link with just that close one-eyed attention a hen might give to a speck of ground corn.

"Great God in Zion," she said, and blushed the color back into her cheeks. "It's Frank Leslie!"

"Nobody but," Link said. "Sit you down, Mother Carrie, and tell me what I can do you for."

Charmian Carew was made of tough stuff. She gave him another sharp, sideways look, nodded, and came and sat down on the straight-back chair beside the bed.

"Now, Frank . . ." she said. "You calling yourself Fred Link these days? Well, I might have known no common saddle-tramp would be killing Ike Stern with a pistol, and that nasty, dirty Coe boy as well." She flounced up her skirts and settled back in the chair. "I came up here to thank the man that saved my poor Charles."

"Charles?" Link didn't know what the hell the old

bat was talking about. "Charlies who?" Did she mean Charlie Coe?

"Sheriff Swazee is who I mean! Charles Swazee. I am Missus Swazee."

Link stared at her for a moment, then leaned back in the pillows biting his lip to keep from laughing. How in God's name had that tough, righteous little old sheriff . . . and Charmian Carew! They were of an age but damn all else they had in common!

"Well, I certainly congratulate you, Char—Mrs. Swazee. The sheriff was a brave fellow."

"Mister Swazee *is* a very brave man, Frank!" Tears were in the old woman's eyes. "Charley Swazee is the best, bravest man I ever knew." She patted her eyes with a ball of crumpled handkerchief. "But I do believe he would be dead now, if you hadn't . . . interfered."

Link refrained from telling her that the old man wouldn't have been hurt at all if Fred Link hadn't provided the occasion for the Coes to jump him. "I only did what any man might do—they were looking for trouble with me, too, you know."

"They almost killed him!" she said. "His poor head is so badly burned."

"He's a hard-case," Link said. "He'll do."

The old woman drew herself up. "Yes, he'll do. And once he's out of his bed, he'll be going straight to Boise to see the Federal Marshal! Then, so help me," her small bony hands shook with rage, "so help me, we'll drive every single dog of a Coe clear out of this country —or hang 'em!"

Nothing funny about the old lady then. Link had a notion it would be hard cheese for any Coe who fell into Charmian Swazee's little bony hands. And, thinking of which, just in case the Coes wouldn't let

109

him get peacefully out of this town . . . "The Coes . . ."

"What of them?"

"I've heard of the old man."

"Anse."

"Yes, and I've met Wilson Coe—doesn't strike me as a fighting man."

"Wilson Coe is a snake in the grass," Charmian Swazee said. "He would steal the pennies off a dead man's eyelids!" She was plucking at the handkerchief in her lap, tugging at the lace. "And Anse Coe is an old devil straight out of hell and needs to be sent right back where he came from!" She gave Link a sudden sideways look. "And somebody's going to do it, sooner than he thinks!"

Link lay back, listening to her. The Coes must have put years of pressure on old Swazee—pushing him, trying him, likely scaring off any deputies the old man got to back him. Doubtful if the sheriff had any power at all outside of town. More a town marshal than anything, and an old, tired town marshal at that. The only way Swazee could have made real trouble for a bunch like the Coes would have been to get killed by them. That would have brought law down from the capital, and damned quick.

It occurred to Link that he'd likely done Mister Anse Coe a considerable favor—if Coe didn't mind losing a trashy son—in saving the sheriff's life. Doubtful if Mister Anse Coe would see it that way, however.

"Young Charlie Coe dead?"

A pleased smile twitched at her mouth. "Died yesterday evening in doctor Mayberry's house." That bird-like eye glanced at Link. "You broke his stomach for him."

"MacDuff says there're two other boys—older brothers."

110

Charmian nodded. "Each worse than the other! Billy Coe shot a man and his wife dead, just outside of town, not a year ago. Just plain murder! And the circuit judge turned his face away. No evidence. And two people saw the murder done!" She put her hand up to her face for a moment, distraught. Link saw her age in that. Nineteen years ago, Charmian Carew would have shrugged off any number of killings—and probably had, in those Fort Arthur cribs she had kept so well supplied. Time, and concern for the tough little sheriff, had taken some of the starch out of her, after all.

"And Reed is worse and quicker with a gun, Frank. Look out for Reed Coe when you fight him! That damn Ichabod looks like butter wouldn't melt in his mouth, but you be careful when you fight him!"

Link observed that the reformed Mrs. Swazee had him fighting this Coe family, root and branch, undoubtedly to solve all the sheriff's problems for him in one blow. It didn't seem to him, particularly as his side and shoulder were hurting him something special, that that was a duty he was bound to undertake.

The reformed Mrs. Swazee went on to press just this point. "Fred," she said, "you can trust me to keep my mouth closed about knowing you before. It's the least that I can do, seeing you saved my Charles."

Link supposed she meant that she'd keep shut just as long as he did. It seemed a reasonable bargain.

"Now, I haven't talked to Charles about it and I know you're too bad hurt to think about it yet yourself —but it seems to me you might be right smart, Fred Link, were you to take a deputy's badge from Mister Swazee, and . . ."

It pained Link's side a great deal to laugh, and he tried to stop it as soon as he could, but it was hard. He'd lie back on the pillows with the laughter

111

thudding against his wounds, and try like hell to think of something else, something besides busted-up old Frank Leslie strolling the town with a badge on his tit. But he couldn't do it. The recurrent picture of it and the outraged hen-face peering at him from the bedside chair would set him off again. Finally it was the gunshot wounds that sobered him. They—especially the wound in his side—began to really hurt, until every chuckle cost him. It slowed the laughter, and then stopped it. He caught his breath, shifted on the pillows, and gently shrugged his left shoulder. The bandage seemed to be binding him.

Charmian Swazee got up out of the chair, and stood to her full five feet of height, looking down at him. "Funny enough, just now," she said, "but maybe not so funny when Reed and Billy Coe get back to this town." It was said with considerable satisfaction.

She stalked off to the bedroom door with her head bobbing walk, turned, and said, "Just the same, I appreciate . . ."

"Oh, hell, Charmian, a favor from one old-timer to another. It was my pleasure."

When the old lady was gone and the door shut behind her, Link twisted carefully in the bed, trying to get his fingers underneath the edge of the bandage on his shoulder. It was way too tight. He could feel it cutting into him, making him feel damn tired. He got a finger under the collar of the nightshirt—must belong to MacDuff—and plucked at the edge of the bandage. Couldn't get the damn thing loose.

The bedroom door opened, and MacDuff stood in the doorway with a double-barrelled shotgun over his arm. "What do you think you're doing there?" he said. "Leave that alone!"

"Too damn tight. It'll be giving me a sepsis!"

"Leave it alone—Mayberry'll be up here in an hour

or so. He's a good sawbones. Leave that to him. You damn near bled out, bartender!" Link took his hand away from the bandage. He could wait an hour.

"What do you want, MacDuff? You going duck hunting with that smoke-pole?"

MacDuff seemed embarrassed. "Some people—me and Mayberry, Addison from the pharmaceutical, and Perry Patterson—well, we're sort of riding shotgun on you up here for a few days 'til you can get up."

"Why, MacDuff! I'm touched!"

"Don't think we mean to get into any shooting scrape with the Coe boys. It's just we figure it'll keep the Rocking-D hands from coming up here to take you out and hang you to a lamp-post! They didn't care for you shooting that cowboy, Evans, down like a dog that way."

"That cowboy had outstayed his welcome," Link said. "Still, I will sleep better knowing there's somebody down there." Odd, how difficult it was for a man to thank people who meant him nothing but good, and were going to some little trouble over it, too.

"Thank those boys for me, MacDuff. I'm . . . I'm beholden to them."

MacDuff grunted. "You want the pot?"

"Yes," Link said. "I'm sorry to say I need that damn pot."

It was seven more days before Link could get up and out of the bed just to sit. Painful days, sometimes, when Doctor Mayberry, a blond little man with a wispy beard, who looked to be about sixteen years old, changed Link's bandages, and in between the changing, cleaned, probed, swabbed and syringed the wounds.

"Nice things," he'd say. "Very nice. Both wounds

clear through and through. And the one through your side just nice enough to miss nicking the bottom of the lung. Didn't strike a rib, either. Very nice. If it had struck a rib, you'd have bone splinters all through your insides!"

Link knew the wounds were through and through because Mayberry had run linen packing in a raveled cord clear through the wounds from front to back, and that cord soaked with carbolic solution. "My solution," Mayberry would say, working away. "'Mayberry's Solution.' I may write it up for the *New England Proceedings!*"

It was an odd sensation, besides the pain, to feel the doctor slowly tugging the packing through his body. There was something oddly wincing, almost pleasurable, about it.

"I must consider Mister Stern to have been a gentleman, of sorts," Mayberry said on one occasion. "No notched leads. Bullets left smooth and round as they came from the box. Stern had something of the gentleman about him, no question . . ."

Seven days of this, and finally more wearing, seven days of nothing much to do. Of lying in bed staring at the ceiling, or one of the old *Police Gazettes* MacDuff had sent in from the barbershop. There were, MacDuff said, people in town who had novels to read, and apparently read them themselves. Had some collections of Shakespeare and plenty of Bibles. But MacDuff didn't know them personally. Would rather not ask someone he didn't know personally for their Shakespeares.

Link had already read the Bible.

He read the *Police Gazette*, ate the good meals the Chinaman set up, and lay in bed feeling his gunshot wounds slowly change from aching to itching. Plenty of time to think.

Plenty to think about.

The past . . . That was a long thought. A dream. A memory of long rides, fast rides through wild country. Of handsome houses and girls who sighed, and wept. Laughing girls who loved the gay life, loved the excitement, the men. Girls who loved the shame of it . . .

A man who hadn't spent at least a few weeks, let alone months, in a high-class whorehouse, was a man who didn't know the true relaxation of pleasure, was also a man who knew less of women than he might otherwise have learned. To observe women in a fine house, was to get if not a complete understanding of them—only a fool ever claimed that—at least a notion of their fears, and angers, and satisfactions.

An education. An education about men, of course, as well. But nothing much there that an honest man didn't already know about himself.

Long, sweet months behind shades, behind fine lace curtains. Months in an air of French scent, and music-box music, and fiddle and piano as well, sometimes. Giggles . . . whispers . . . tears . . . screams of rage or fear. Groans of pleasure. The soft murmure of kitchen chatter, wry remarks about men. Rich laughter . . . The smell of them. That rich, permeating odor of powder and flesh, and, usually in the same two or three days, at breakfast, the dark, oyster smell—just a trace—of their periodics.

Sometimes trouble in those houses. Just enough trouble for a young hard-case to keep his hands in. As far as Link knew, unless one fellow had died from a broken head, he had never had to kill a man in a sporting house.

In the back yard, once. But that had been something else . . . a different matter of business.

There might, he supposed, be something better for a man that such a stay. A long hunt in high country was

115

in some ways as good, he thought. Better yet, if a man could so divide his time that he alternated, say three months boarding at a prime house (a new house each time, of course) and follow that with a long hunt in the mountains. After elk, or mountain goat. A long, long hunt, climbing up alongside a small river, camping beside it every night, for the clear, icy water . . . the fish. Cook them split on a stick, leaning close to the flames—not too close—and you needed nothing on the cooked fish except a scraping of salt off the little lump in the pack. You needed just that, and, if you had the fixings, a dutch oven lid of sourdough biscuits. Those two things to eat, a cold, clear night, with clouds of stars over the mountains, and a couple of Hudson Bay's to roll up in for sleeping—that was what was needed, that was the sort of night to spend high in the mountains, hunting elk.

Link had had those pleasures. More than months spent in houses here and there—pleasure heightened by the money that flowed in. Quim money—slippery and sweet to spend. The clothes he had had made for himself with that money! What a jackass dandy he must have looked, with his lace-front shirts, his fine worsted trousers cut tight enough to show his parts . . . fine gold watches, chimes and all, calenders, too, a couple of them. Boots as black as tar and as soft as butter. Fancy pearl-handle pistols, left most of those in the dresser drawer. Dressing gowns—one made of coarse-woven silk on the island of Japan. By God, that one was a beautiful thing . . . trees woven right into it. A scene of trees with white birds sitting in the branches . . . Susy Crank had given him that. What the hell did she give him that for? He'd never taken her to bed, that was for sure: Susy had loved ladies, except for strictly business. Ah, he'd gotten her Sis out of Ella's place! That was it. Beautiful robe. Commodore

116

Vanderbilt couldn't have bought a better thing to wear.

Yes, he'd had those whorehouse pleasures. Had the pleasure of romances in those houses, as well. Screwing, to be sure, but romances as well, for whores are as lovely as any woman can be as long as that loving is not for money. Been loved, and done some loving of his own. Sometimes, when there seemed to be no reason for it, he would remember a girl's eyes. Diana, at Mrs. Robbin's, she'd had soft, smoke-grey eyes. A dreamy smile to go with those eyes . . .

Almost any woman is more than enough treasure for a man. He'd handled those treasures like bolts of cloth at a drygoods store—the feel of them, sometimes, came back to his fingertips. And he'd handled them roughly, too, as any mack must, but he'd never crippled one, never made one ugly. Not much to boast of, he supposed.

He'd had that life, and the wild life, too. Running stolen horses—not the same thing as stealing them. Ran them down to Old Mexico with Ramon Piedras and his brother. A hell of a ride. They'd thought the posse long since quit, and damned if two men— fellows that had owned the horses, they supposed— those two fellows had ridden after them more than eight hundred miles and peppered them more than smartly at the river. Sons-of-guns had crossed first and lay waiting. Rifle-fight ensued, as the cavalry put it for the newspapers after their Indian chases. Ramon's brother shot out of his saddle like a rabbit and the horse-herd going one way and Frank and Ramon the other. Ramon. That was one fellow whose whereabouts Link knew: ran a boat yard in Vera Cruz. You'd think that river-crossing would have soured him on watery doings. Not a bit.

They'd caught up just three horses from that herd on

the Texas side of the river. Three horses, for all that riding. That was the trip made a saloon gambler and ladies' man out of Frank Leslie. Damn sure wasn't going to be any cowboy, after all that riding.

Lot of hunting, too. Guided hunting, for a while. That was another kind of memory, the kind that hurt when it slid into your head. Those fool Russians . . . that damn fool old Indian. And Mister Frank Leslie maybe the biggest fool of all. The sound of his horse's hooves ringing on the cobbles at the Gunstock stables. She'd tried to hold on . . . held on to the stirrup leathers as he rode out. Gone now, and best forgotten.

Best forgotten. Best left in the might-have-beens, along with a little reformed whore at a mountain ranch . . . a ranch at a river. Meadows where the Appaloosas grazed the Spring grass.

Best forgotten. All best forgotten—the other ranch woman, and her rough old foreman. Best not remembered. Better not.

Gunfights?

Link lay for hours one warm, sunny afternoon— that damn winter done at last, it looked like—and watched the year's first couple of flies buzzing around the open window not quite daring to fly outside. Outside must look very big to them.

For several hours, Link had lain in bed feeling a little tired, maybe, but that was all, and tried to remember the fights he had had with guns. Some knives, too. Guns and knives were easy to remember. He didn't bother with fists, the number of times he'd fallen onto fisticuffs and gotten thrashed, too, a few times. Always seemed so damn embarrassing, hitting a man in the face. He'd a damn sight rather shoot a fellow!

Bit fight with that Englishman, though. A hell of a

fight. Surprised he could remember that one, hard as he was hit!

Otherwise, it was guns and knives . . .

He remembered them all, counted them up, and when he'd thought about them, Link was most surprised that he hadn't been killed long ago. Should have been, that was for certain. He'd been hit, though. Though not so badly, most of the time, as Stern and the Coe boy had shot him up. This last time . . . He wondered why he'd felt the way he had when Stern hadn't fired at him at the last. Perhaps he shouldn't have killed the cowboy—MacDuff had told him his name; what the hell was it . . .?

Perhaps he shouldn't have killed the man. God knows it was murder. Fellow'd gone over like a snapped Jack on a plain deal.

Probably should have left him alone. Already knocked him ass over teakettle, broken his nose . . .

Gun-proud. Proud of his skill. Happy to be so brave that he could face gunfire most men wouldn't dare to. Well, it was true. In those short seconds—much less than seconds, usually—he stood in all that smoke and noise, heard every bullet that went signing by him— saw everything, almost everybody's face every instant. Everybody moved so slowly except for him. He moved quickly and did everything he wanted.

It was like being God Almighty for a moment. Or Prince Satan, his mother would have said, amid the storms of hell.

Pride . . . that sin by which the angels fell. Men who couldn't do that . . . men who hadn't done it . . . would never understand.

It was the most overpowering pleasure. Women. The sweet breaths taken on a windy day. The blackest pipes of opium in any den on the Coast. None of them

119

held quite such pleasures, such sharpening of the edge of life.

He'd seen that in Stern's eyes, he realized. That was the look they'd shared. The glance he'd shared with others, too, before a shooting.

Anticipation. A shared pleasure, a great and over-powering pleasure coming soon for them both.

To be sure, he'd often been afraid. More than afraid, sometimes. It was, he thought, lying against the pillows, watching the play of sunlight against the window frame, it was that that afforded such great pleasure.

Difficult to break a habit of that sort when pride was in it, too. When you could see this time and your time passing so quickly. Soon, there'd be no place in the West out of sound of the railroad's whistle, carpenter's hammers, steam engines and mining machinery. Already a man couldn't ride where he pleased from Canada to Old Mexico. Be stopped at a hundred fence lines, and County Lines, and Township lines. Soon enough, a man would have to put his horse on a railroad train, pick it up the other end of the trip.

Sounded funny but it was true. And it had all happened so quickly. When he was a boy, hell, there had been no end to it. Buffalo on buffalo grass for two thousand miles, cattle just coming to the high country.

A person knew everybody in those days. Now, most of the men you met were strangers. That had been happening since the war, of course. More and more.

Link remembered shooting that big Irishman, the one in the plug hat. *Would hate to have fist-fought that fellow. He would have broken my bones . . .* Some city hoodlum, likely, a man from one of the big gangs in New York, perhaps. He'd had that clever city look about him, like a great Barbary ape with a nasty secret. The Rabbits . . . the Gophers . . . One of those gangs.

Been some Sidney Ducks out in San Francisco. Nice fellows, those he knew. As long as you didn't have anything they wanted.

It was an odd thing. As he remembered those men, the ones he had fought, and often enough killed, he remembered them alive. The way they'd looked—that quiet, small man at Gunstock; Shannon, his name had been. And an old Missouri-border gunman—Link remembered him sitting his horse up at Rifle River, remembered the old man's measured way of talking. And a laughing red-headed gunfighter with a quiet brother.

Link remembered those and twenty seven others.

Too damn many.

But he remembered them alive. He didn't like picturing them dead. What it came to was that many of them might have been his friends, if things had fallen out differently. They had, after all, a great deal in common.

Thirteen days after the fight, Link was up for more than sitting.

He wasn't going far, just about his room most of the day, with two slow trips downstairs when the place was fairly empty. On those trips downstairs, he got some looks, but not too many. People weren't that sure of him and they were damn sure of the Coes. Of what the Coes would surely do, in their own good time, to the bartender who had shot the guts out of Charlie Coe, and that temperamental fat boy only eighteen years old.

They gave Link looks—admiring, some of them. But no one bought him a whiskey.

He wasn't feeling up to drinking it, anyway. That first day up, Link was glad enough to see end. He skipped the supper of fried liver and onions that the Chinaman sent up, and slid between the sheets of that familiar bed with a groan of relief. His side felt as if it'd been beaten with sticks.

He slept deep, though, and the next day felt much better.

The third day he spent on his feet, in and around the place. Nobody seemed to notice him out in front of the Rose where he stood leaning against a sun-warmed wall, enjoying the noise and bustle of the street. No one troubled him there; just as well. The Bisley hung from his gunbelt as heavy as an anvil. It would likely have taken him both hands to pull it from the holster.

Some young boys did come by, though, after school hours. He figured they must have been haunting the White Rose from day to day to get a look at him. This was an old story and one that he had once enjoyed, to have boys trailing after him in the street, looking in the windows when he went to a restaurant, or to a barber shop to get his hair cut. All that had once been enjoyable; now, it only bored and troubled him.

The boys lounged across the street and stared at him, and whispered and nudged one another.

Link paid no attention to them. He leaned against the rough plank wall, feeling the warmth of the wood through his shirt. He was thinking about getting out of town.

And not much time left to do it.

The old Chinaman had been bad enough, knowing him, knowing his name—had seen him shoot a man, for God's sake! But the old man seemed to be no fool and if he'd been all there was to worry about, Link would have been content enough to stay put, and raid poor MacDuff's cash-box for a gambling stake.

But then came the fight. Bad as any gun fight could be—bound to bring people around to gawk at him, just as the town boys were staring at him now. The fight alone, was more than enough reason for Buckskin Frank Leslie, changed name or not, to get the hell out of Colt Creek. Charmian Carew—Swazee, as she was now—just topped it, as the lumberjacks say. Topped it right off.

Time to go. And that taking no account of those two Coe boys, brothers, coming up-trail. Those boys made it time to hurry.

He thought he'd give it one more day. Just one more day to rest up, see if he could get Mayberry to stop poking and pushing at that damn hole in his side. It was almost closed now, and no bad pus coming out of it. If Mayberry'd just leave it alone. The shoulder *was* closed. Only a red sort of scab, where the bullet had started through. Same thing on the back, the back of his shoulder. He saw that in the mirror over the highboy dresser.

CHAPTER 9

NEXT MORNING, he felt good, the best he had since the shooting, and determined to get the hell out of Colt Creek, before he had to shoot his way out.

Mayberry made a morning visit, and poked and pried at both wounds somewhat less than usual. He put a light bandage on each one, and said, with some apparent regret, "They'll do."

Link had been worried about paying the man—it would be a considerable bill for sure—but finally just asked Mayberry straight out.

"You would owe me thirty or forty dollars for the work I've done on you," the healer said, "and I ought to charge you more for killing Coe and Stern—they sent me a fair amount of business week in and week out; still, I suppose the shooting must be called a public service, and since you undoubtedly can't pay the bill anyway, we'll call it a charity matter."

There's no use hitting a doctor, Link thought. You might as well hit a door-post, for all the good it would do you. "I'll pay that forty dollars when I can, Doc."

"As you wish," Mayberry said. He didn't look to be expecting the cash soon.

When Mayberry'd left, Link got out of bed, dressed

—the fat girls had cleaned his clothes and put them away in the dresser—and strapped on the Bisley Colt's. The revolver didn't feel quite as heavy today.

Then he gathered the rest of his possibles—not much, at that—packed his war-bag, and walked out of the room, the Henry balanced in his hand. Strange, how it felt a little sad to be leaving. God knows the town hadn't been much to him—a place to get out of the cold, mainly, have some hot food, shelter, a chance to wrangle a small card-stake . . . Well, he'd gotten those, though not much time to build a stake. And he'd had the girl, poor creature that she was. And he'd had a gunfight. Nothing new in that. And been nicely ventilated. Nothing much new in that, either. Play with knives, you will be cut.

MacDuff was starting up the stairs as Link started down. "Up?" he said. "And going, too, by the look of it." They met in the middle of the stair. The Rose was morning empty.

"I owe you a good deal, MacDuff," Link said. "A large part of it from my own cash drawer, I suspect," MacDuff said, trying to give Link a hard look. "But I can't fault you for clearing out of this town. You stay, and Anse Coe'll have you killed—likely hung up to a beam like a dog."

"I'll send you some money, when I make it—for the bed, and the care . . ."

"You'll send me nothing," MacDuff said. "You tended my bar better than it's ever been done, you beat one rogue who needed a beating, and you shot two killers down who needed that as well. As far as your killing that drover there at the end . . . Well, why not? The fellow lay down with dogs, he got up with fleas, and that's that!"

"Well, thank you, anyway." Link hesitated a moment, then said, "If you get into trouble over this,

125

MacDuff . . . trouble over me staying here shot up, you send somebody down to La Passe. Likely I'll be trying for a job down there. You send somebody, and I'll come up." He hadn't said a thing like that in some long time. He was surprised to hear himself saying it now.

MacDuff got red in the face. "Now, now," he said, "I won't get caught in a wheel about it. I'll tell 'em I was scared to do otherwise; the Coes, I guess, don't have any great opinion of my guts, anyway. You go on, now. Get movin'."

One of the fat girls, Link didn't know which one, came out on the saloon floor and hugged him goodbye. She smelled of sweat and lily of the valley. He saw the Chinaman standing back in the kitchen corridor, and waved to the old man when the girl let him go. The old man just looked at him; didn't wave back.

Link had wanted to say goodbye to the girl—he'd meant to talk to Mayberry about her, about her fits, but he hadn't been able to say anything for fear Mayberry'd pick up right away what he'd had to do with her. An embarrassment had kept him from a mention he should have made.

She was nowhere to be seen at the stable. Beanpole Patterson had taken a last two-bits from him, and then gone stilting into the stable to saddle and lead out the brown. No limp. The animal looked better than it had since Willow Falls. You couldn't call it lively, but it did look some better. Link recalled that Patterson had been one of the men who'd sat shotgun while he was hurt.

"Understand you sat up at the Rose for me with a shotgun, Mister Patterson."

Beanpole flushed with pleasure. "Us Confederates,"

he said, "stick close together. The Coes have had their own Yankee way here long enough!"

"Right you are, sir," Link said, reached up for the horn and hauled himself up into the saddle—and damn glad to be sitting, after the long walk from the saloon. "Damn right."

He thumped the brown with his heal, and guided the horse out of the stable yard, turning back to throw a sort of salute to Patterson, who returned it, looking very pleased. And on out into the street, a street on a cool, sunny morning, a street with a different aspect when a man is mounted, even if poorly, rather than trudging through knee-deep mud.

Link had a slight ache in his side to keep him reminded, but even so, he felt uncommon well. The long bed rest had done more than heal his wounds; it had rested him deeper, gotten the trail weariness, that year-long exhaustion, out of his bones.

He relaxed to the brown's habitual lurching gate—like a camel, the Laredo banker, an honest man, had said at the sale—and watched the folks of Colt Creek bustling through their town. Watched a pretty girl, a nice girl, walking the boardwalk with a child, hand in hand. Hers, or a little brother? A little brother, Link supposed, saw no flash of gold on the girl's finger.

Two horsemen were coming toward him on the left, hard-looking men. As they drew near, he saw they wre drovers, with work-broken hands and deep range holsters. Laboring men, not gun-sports. It seemed that Billy Coe and Reed Coe would be coming home too late to take a hand, too late to exercise a revenge for the fat boy's death.

Link couldn't say he was sorry. One hard fight and over two weeks in bed sick as a horse was more than enough. As to the Coes' style of reaching for a fellow with a long arm as they had, supposedly, with that freighter fellow, well, a change-name drifter is hard to find. A lot of men in the West with scars on their cheeks, men his age. Even a few fancied the Bisley model in the Colt's. No, the Coes would have to look hard to find hide or hair of Fred Link.

And, of course, if they did find him . . . well, his luck had held against fiercer fellows than those two were likely to be.

He was near the edge of town now, just passed a house with a sow and litter grunting in the front yard. He put spurs to the brown, and as it raised its pace to a jolting trot, he stood a little in his stirrups to ease the trouble in his side.

He pulled the brown up on a rise to the east of town, overlooking the stock yards. He had meant to come out for a visit, do a Boston walk, and the way his side was aching, that might have been the better notion. He sat the standing horse, stretching a little in the saddle, trying to ease the knot there, just under his ribs. Sore as a saddle-boil.

Two of the men working down there chousing a bunch of steers through a feed-lot gate saw him on the rise, and waved. He could see their faces, but didn't recognize them. Then he heard his name shouted. They'd recognized him from the Rose, maybe from the fight. They were waving to him, and it was a mighty temptation to ride the brown on down there, climb out of the confounded saddle, and maybe share a noon time beefsteak with those boys, stink and all. A mighty temptation.

But if you're going it's best to go.

He waved back at he men below, kicked the brown back into its damned trot, and went on his way, up a narrow, slowly rising track toward distant hills, low enough, thank God, not to have any winter snow still lying along their crests. He'd try to get over those, at least before he made camp. But it would be an early camp, that was for certain sure. If it wasn't for his side, he might have done a good day's ride, even with so late a start, gotten well over those hills, and then gone some more, until he found a nice break, with willows and a creek, bent himself a hogan with the willows, built a little fire before it, and have been in Redskin heaven for the night.

Now it looked as though he'd be lucky to scale the hills before his left side called a halt. He'd have to roll in his blanket in the open air. Be better than jolting on this damn brown, anyhow.

Might be he was thinking too much of his comfort.

Could have been how they got so close, while he sat dreaming away like a Pipe-man.

Three men had ridden over a ridge not two hundred yards away, plain as the nose on your face and were heading down toward him at an easy trot. They had rifles across their saddle bows.

Link pulled the brown up, reached down to the saddle boot, and pulled the Henry free. He hated rifle fighting and was not wonderfully good at it, either.

The three of them were coming on close enough for him to make out their faces, now. Drovers. No question of that. Cowboys mounted on ranch stock. Link couldn't see the brands, but he would have bet they marked out Rocking D's, every one. He levered a round into the Henry's receiver, and turned a little in his saddle for easier shooting.

Three to one was heavy odds especially with rifles. On another sort of horse, he might have run for it. Not on the brown.

Suddenly, a shout away, the three drovers pulled up. They kept their rifles across their saddle bows.

Then one, the leader, cupped his hands, and called to Link.

"Say, rider! You Link?"

Link saw no reason and no use denying it.

"That's my name! What's your business with me?"

The leader took his hat off, and waved it back toward town. "Mister Coe says you're to get back to town there!"

The shout made a slight echo off the slopes behind him.

Link sat for a moment, thinking about it.

For a moment, he thought the drovers were pulling some rag to run him back into an ambush. Then he thought again. It did appear that Mister Anse Coe intended that Link go back to Colt Creek so that an example could be made of him, right there. It was an interesting notion, and increased Link's respect for the man.

An upstart barkeeper shoots his son down and then tries to run out of town. Tries, but doesn't make it. Is turned back like a coyote run by greyhounds, turned back and trapped, waiting for the hunters.

The Coe boys must be due in a few days, and since it's a family matter, it must be attended to by family. No using a pack of drovers against that bartender, if it can be avoided. Make an example. Show the town what happens to a man who gets lucky with a revolver against a Coe. A nice idea, bound to increase the town's respect and fear. Except that the coyote is no coyote at all.

He's a wolf.

Link leveled the Henry and shot the lead drover out of his saddle. The man hit hard but his foot twisted and held in the stirrup, and the cowpony bucked and reared, and ran.

Link spurred the brown to confuse their aim, and

130

did his damndest to hold a bead on one of the drovers still up. The cowboy had his own rifle raised, and Link saw out of the corner of his eye the other mounted drover galloping headlong after the man being dragged. It seemed to Link to be a waste of time.

He and the cowboy fired together. Link missed cold, but the brown gasped and staggered as it took a hit. Link levered the Henry and balanced himself as best he could on the stumbling horse, trying to keep his head dead on the drover's belly.

Then he was down. Down hard and rolling to avoid the brown's flailing hooves. His side—the pain knifed through him. But he hadn't been hit. A volley of fire came from behind him, aimed at his horse.

Link started to twist to his other side, to free his revolver—when he stopped dead still and lay looking up at one of the drovers. The man had a Winchester rifle leveled down at him.

Even then, Link might have made a try; the drover looked mighty upset, was weeping, in fact. Link might have made the try, but he heard hoofbeats, and looked up the slope where the sound was coming from.

Three horsemen were riding down on them, all with rifles out and across their saddles.

Link heard the brown groan and die just down the slope. This waddie and the others riding to him had shot the animal down from choice. Could've as easily done for him.

Four to one. Bad odds.

"You damn murderin' son-of-a-bitch!" The drover already leveled on him was blubbering like a babe. "You killed Perce Baxter—was a better man than you'll ever be, you dirty scar-face son of a damn pig!"

The fellow looked mad enough to kill, and likely would with his friends coming up to give him the sand.

"Perce, huh?" Link said up to the fellow. "He

looked more like a Mary-Ann, to me. Your bunk-house gal, was he?" And he prepared to jerk the Colt's and kill the crybaby.

"Raise that rifle, Bucky!" A big voice, and a big man sounding it. The three horsemen pulled up, damn near on top of Link. "Raise it up, I said!" The Big man leaned forward out of his saddle, and knocked the muzzle of the drover's Winchester aside. "We got orders here, God damnit!"

Another of the cowboys looked down at Link; he was grinning. "Was I you, Pilgrim," he said, "I'd take my hand away from that fancy pistol, or we're likely to have us an accident with you, orders or not."

Link took his hand off the Colt's.

"He killed Perce!" the crying drover said.

"I figured he had," said the big man. He was older than the others, and carried a fine walrus mustache and a round potbelly that looked to be all muscle.

"Well, Cap," said the grinning cowboy, "what do them orders say we got to do right now?"

The big man stared down at Link, and Link could see from his eyes and the red flush in his face that he'd be just as happy to set his men loose. Baxter must have been a likeable fellow. But the big man bit his lip, and mastered himself.

"Gun-fighter," he said. "Mister Coe has told us off to patrol the town—"

"Middle of Spring gather, too," the grinning cowboy said.

"—to patrol this town," the big man continued, "and to keep you from getting out of it."

"Do tell," Link said, trying to look relaxed and at ease lying in the dirt at their horses' hooves. "Fears he'll miss me when I'm gone?" The grinning cowboy laughed.

"You're not going to be gone, Mister Whatever-your-name-is!" the big man said. "That's just it. You're stickin' right here in Colt Creek, until some fellows get in here from Boise, and that won't be long. Got some family business with you, those fellows have."

Link could see now what Anse Coe was after and it made him feel considerable respect for the old devil. Somebody'd had the luck, or the guts, to gun a son of his, and the old man obviously intended to make a lesson of that person. To hold him in the town and have him killed in the town, like a trapped rabbit. By Coes. It would be something for Colt Creek to remember.

Link smiled up at the potbelly. "I'd say your old boss is a humdinger," he said.

The big man looked down at him for a moment, surprised. Then he nodded. "You are damned right about that, Gunfighter," he said.

"For Jesus' sake, Cap, can't we even rope-whip this son-of-a-bitch?" It was the crybaby cowboy.

"You try runnin' again," the big man said to Link. "You try runnin' again, we will whip the hide right off you." He leaned back in his saddle, and his horse, a heavy-set grey, shifted with his weight. "Mister Coe said to just send you back this time—" he looked up at his men, "—and that's what we're goin' to do."

"What about his guns?" The fourth drover. A dark man, with his long black hair twisted into pigtails. A breed of some kind.

"He keeps 'em," the big man said, and the drovers shifted restlessly in their saddles. "He keeps 'em! Orders." And to Link, "Now, Mister, get up out of that dirt, and go collect your tack off that horse. Then you get to walkin' back to town. Don't you come back this way or any other way outside the town, day or night, or you'll sure get a whippin', or worse."

"We ought to burn him. We'll burn you, you son-of-a-bitch!" The weeping drover had dried his tears.

"We can brand him, I'll bet," the breed said. "I'll bet Mister Coe wouldn't mind if we branded his face for him. I could take the nose right off him . . ."

"All right now—that's enough," the big man said. And Link, figuring it was getting to be time to move off, got up, favoring his sore side, which felt damn near split open by his fall, and walked stiffly down to the brown to go to work loosening the cinch. It had occurred him also that if he could get to the right distance from the drovers—and at the right angle—he might just be able to kill the lot of them. Likely not, of course; four to one was stretching hard. But it might be worth a try . . .

The brown was lying heavy on the off stirrup leathers, and it took some considerable hauling to pull the outfit free. Link had just bent to unbuckle the bridle when he heard horses running. He looked up and saw two riders up along the ridge, about a quarter mile away. Drovers, sure as hell.

And that busted the bull's back for sure. One against four was a stretch; against six, it was a no-hoper.

Link gathered his outfit, saddle, bridle, war-bag, and looked around for the Henry. "Hey! Your rifle's up here!" The grinning cowboy. Link walked back up the slope to get it, trying to walk easily, as though there was nothing wrong with his side. All he could do now was to keep his mouth shut and his head down and get the hell out.

The two riders were down from the ridge now, coming toward them. One of them was shouting something.

"Says Chico's caught Perce up an' he's a goner," said the breed.

Link looked for the fallen Henry, saw it, and went

to pick it up. Then he turned, and went back down the slope for the rest of his things. A word wrong, now, or maybe just any word at all, and it was likely the drovers would kill him, Potbelly or not.

As he gathered his gear up, wrestling the damn heavy saddle up onto his shoulders, slinging bridle and war-bag over his arm, all the while keeping a grip on the Henry with his other hand, Link listened carefully to the tone of the cowboys' talk behind him.

He listened especially for a sudden silence.

That would mean they'd decided, orders or not, to put him down. Time then to drop this load of stuff, go for the Colt's, and see if he could manage to hit one or two of those boys before he checked out.

But there was no silence. The boys were complaining, back there, arguing withe the big man. They were complaining, arguing. But they weren't *doing*.

Looked like sore-side Fred Link would see another sunrise. He humped his back up to try and make the load ride easier, and stepped out, heading back to the stock yards and Colt Creek. And by God, he missed the brown. Only a few yards walked, and his bad side felt on fire. Damn horse . . . put him, put that idiot girl to all that trouble throwing out a splint, is nicely doctored up, and gets himself shot dead not twenty minutes out of town. Damn animal! Link knew the drovers were watching him stagger along, figuring him for an old poop well past it. Could be the reason they hadn't shot him. Sorry for him.

He straightened his back and tried to stride out, trying to keep the load balanced, so it wouldn't drag at him, twist at his side and hurt that damn wound so much.

It was going to be a long walk, just getting out of their sight. A hell of a long walk. And no looking back.

Too damn long. Not two hundred yards walking, and Link could feel his breakfast heaving in his guts. The whole track was wavering while he looked at it and sweat was running off his face like rain.

He just kept hauling one foot out in front of the other—out in front, and down, and lean on it, and swing the other one out. He'd stumbled twice, certain sure that if he dropped this load, he'd never be able to pick the bastards up.

One of the drovers called something after him. Something funny, it must have been, because he heard the others laugh. He didn't feel any more pain in his side, and thanked God for that. Didn't know if it was bleeding or what and didn't care, long as it didn't hurt. They must have had someone watching that livery, rode out to warn them when he got the brown. If only he had a good horse . . . if only he knew the country around the town. Then, by God, let's see those fence-menders try and keep him from moonlighting out any damn night he chose, patrols or not. Let's see that . . .

But he didn't have a good horse, didn't have any at all, now. And he didn't know the damned countryside, either. Thank God that wound had quit hurting. Must have come near a mile, by now. Near a mile . . .

He'd need an ace, in town. And where the hell to get one? No friend—no serious gun-friend, anyway. MacDuff and the others . . . nice people . . . couldn't go getting them killed up against real badmen. No edge at all in town . . . nothing to make the Coes even bother to come straight at him. Why should they? They could wait for him to show his back—eating, going out to the necessary, crossing the street. And when they had good sight of his back, why, just fire away and break it. No need to take the chances of a fair fight. No one would give a damn how bad a no-name drifter went.

If there was only some way to force them to make a straight fight of it . . . something so they'd have to give him his break, and call it even. Be able to blame him, then, for his own killing . . .

This walking thing, now, this wasn't as bad as it had been. Getting used to it, was all. Having trouble seeing, with all this sweat in his eyes, that's all. Damn near into town by now, probably . . .

Something ws tugging at his toe—and then his side hurt very badly.

No wonder he'd tripped and fallen. Two men were messing with him, pulling him up or something! He heard water shaking in a canteen. Link squeezed his eyes shut, blinked them, trying to clear his vision. He saw a glare of green—the brush along the ridge—and then Bed Packard's face. The stock yard man was kneeling beside him, helping hold him up. Another stock man was holding a canteen up for Link to drink from.

"Hey, Bud . . ."

"Mister Link, you feelin' better?"

Good God almighty . . . fainted away like a girl in school! Link felt so ashamed that tears ached in his eyes. He held up his hand to them, as if the sunlight were bothering him.

"Want some more water, Mister?"

Link shook his head. The men didn't say anything more to him for a minute, and he sat there, taking deep breaths, and began to feel better. Bud Packard was a steady customer at the Rose—beer and Port wine, liked the wine with a chip of ice in it—a quiet enough fellow as those men went.

"We saw those rannies shoot down your horse, Mister

137

Link," Packard said. "Thought they'd damn well killed you, too."

"You got one of them, though," the other stockman said. "You showed them horse-backers a thing or two right there!"

"Wonder they didn't kill you," Packard said. "Those being Rocking-D men, an' what happened at the Rose an' all . . ."

"That fall off the horse hurt you, huh?" the other man said.

"Bad enough," Link said. "I'm obliged to you boys for coming 'round. Give me a hand up."

They helped him to his feet, and he was able to stand all right. His side hurt him, but not too badly. Link saw his saddle and gear scattered all over the track, where he'd taken his Brody, but when he started in to picking the stuff up, Packard stopped him. "No need for you to do that; we'll get it. Got a buckboard coming out from the yards . . . take you right into town, Mister Link."

Was a time he'd have shrugged that buckboard off, shouldered his possibles again, and walked on in. But that long, long ago time now seemed to him to have been before the expulsion from paradise.

CHAPTER 10

THEY TOOK him to the door of the Rose, and Packard climbed down with him, and helped carry his gear inside.

Then Link had to go back outside with Packard, and thank him again, and shake his hand and the other man's as well, and see them get turned around in the narrow street, and then rolling on their way back out of town to the yards.

When Link stepped back in to the Rose, MacDuff was coming down the balcony stairs.

"Well, Jesus God Almighty! Look what the cat dragged back in here!"

Several men at the bar turned for a look, and Link heard someone calling in the back of the place.

"I thought you were to hell and gone, man!" MacDuff looked worried.

"Little problem on the trail . . ." Link said, not caring much if the men at the bar heard him. It would be all over Colt Creek soon enough. "Some Rocking-D riders hated to see me go."

"Son-of-a-bitch," MacDuff said, and came slowly on down the stairs. "Son-of-a-bitch." He walked up to

Link, taking a good look at him as he came. "Shooting?"

"Just a tad."

MacDuff sighed. "And here I thought I was out of it. Link, you are sure as cow's shit goin' to get me killed." He shook his head. "At least, I'll go bossin' a fine bartender."

"No."

MacDuff raised one eyebrow, like an actor.

"I have other plans," Link said, "but I thank you for the compliment." He motioned to his goods. "If you'll rent that room upstairs to me, I'd appreciate it if you'd have those put back up there."

"Hell, yes," MacDuff said. "But how the hell are you goin' to find rent money, except out of my cash box?"

"I'm taking up another line of work, MacDuff. Where does Sheriff Swazee live?"

"But that old man can't help you! The sheriff's in his bed, and damned unlikely ever to get out of it."

"Where does he live, MacDuff?"

There had been many times Link had thanked God he'd changed his name, times the handle Buckskin Frank Leslie would have dumped him deeper into trouble than any man could pull himself out of. Been grateful for that change many times and for the grey in his hair and scar on his cheek as well.

Never more grateful than right now, while strolling along Bartholomew Street in Colt Creek in the bright Spring sunshine. God—if he met someone who knew him . . .

He tried to get his mind of it, to concentrate on the weather, for example. And a beautiful day it was. Spring here at last, no question about that. And none too soon. You would often see a perfect cloudless sky further south—in Arizona, say, or New Mexico. Seen many days like that down there . . . not so common in the mountains, though. Usually were some sort of clouds in mountain skies.

Not today, though. No sir, not today. Fine weather. Really fine.

Few people looking at him as he went walking by. Not many. No way for them to know how funny it was, what they were seeing.

He went down the boardwalk steps and out into the street, cutting across to Main. It seemed to him that a lot of people *were* looking at him—give him a glance, then fall to talking with their friends.

Could be his imagination. Maybe. Not that he'd blame them. Well, if it put a spud up the Coes, it was worth it. Not likely they'd be back-shooting, now. Have to make a fight of it, if only to call him a gun-mad hard-case who had to be put down.

God knew it wasn't much—couldn't really call it an edge. But it was the best he'd been able to do. No vomit an old dog won't eat, was what it amounted to. Ugly, but true enough.

He climbed the steps on the other side of Main Street, and commenced to stroll, not very slowly, down the block toward the Rose. He'd be happy to take MacDuff's horse-laugh in exchange for just getting off the street.

He had just threaded through a crowd standing in front of a saloon called the Lucky Seven, when he felt a hard hand take him by the right arm from behind and yank him hard around.

Link went with the pull, and faster than the pull. He didn't struggle to draw his gun. He ducked, reached way down and across with his left hand and was just able to slide the Arkansas toothpick out of his right boot as he came full around. It was done as

141

nicely as a circus trick. He hadn't had to think about it at all.

He'd intended to stab the fellow in the crotch then. But he couldn't. There was no proper crotch to stab.

It was a dress.

Link hesitated with the knife in his hand and nothing to do, looked up, and received a very hard full-swing punch that struck him on the nose.

Some man standing nearby laughed, and some others, too. Then, when they saw the badge, the laughter died. Link—he could feel his nose throbbing from the punch—stared mighty furious at a girl. Round-faced, stocky, still pale with anger, she, like the others, was staring at his badge.

It was a small six pointed star, polished brass. Said: *Marshal* in small letters. *Colt Creek* in even smaller letters below that. It was just a deputy's badge.

"I'm sorry . . ." the girl began, then her face flushed, and she raised her eyes and stared into his face. "No," she said. "I'm not! You're the son-of-a-bitch dumped me in that trough!"

Some of the loafers standing around whistled at that. They'd thought her a lady, or near to it. Now they'd heard the cursing, they figured she was a whore.

She was dressed well enough. No shirt and trousers, no coachman's vest today. She wore a dark dress, and a lady's straw hat with a small stuffed bluebird sitting up in it. She had a veil, but it was pulled back. She was a short girl, strong-looking rather than fat, with a pretty, round face and big, intelligent grey eyes. As Link recalled lifting her prior to throwing her in the trough, she had a considerable pair of tits to her.

The loafers were laughing now, making remarks about her and the new deputy, as well. It appeared to be a real good time to get off the street and get off as

142

well. He couldn't go around Colt Creek ducking this coach-driving female. He'd be laughed right out from under this damn badge.

Charmian Swazee, the old axe, had been mighty triumphant at the swearing-in. That had been a scene right off the theatre stage. Old Swazee sitting up in bed glowering away; he knew a sporting man when he saw one. And two city councilors, both of them scared as mice about the Coes. One, a banker named Nordstrom, had barely been able to sign the appointment paper, his hand was shaking so much. Give old Charmian credit, she'd gotten a gun to front Sheriff Swazee. Hadn't had to blackmail him into it, either. The Coes had pushed Link behind this damn badge.

Hard to see how he could sink lower than this. Most lawmen Link had known were only outlaws without the guts to go it all. Paid bullies playing decent citizens. He'd known exceptions: Bill Tilghman, Tom Smith . . . Not many.

Well, if you have the name . . .

He reached out, took the girl by the arm, spun her, doubled the arm up behind her back, and frog-marched her off down the boardwalk toward Swazee's little jail, while the loafers roared along behind them.

"You," Link said to her, "are under arrest for assaulting an officer of the law."

Said it, and kept his face straight.

He had the key to Swazee's office and used it, though the girl gave him a tussle there at the door, and pushed her on inside. There was the office not much bigger than a clothes closet, and two small cells beyond it. The cells were only small strong rooms with narrow sheet-iron doors. He shoved the girl into the cell on the left, pulled the door to, and slid the bar across it. There was a big old padlock to hold the bar,

143

but Link wasn't sure he had the key to that, so he didn't snap it closed. Didn't seem necessary, anyway.

"You dirty son-of-a-bitch," the girl said from inside the cell. Her voice was muffled, but Link could make it out.

He could make out the noise outside, for sure. A bunch of lay-abouts were clustering outside the dusty office windows, laughing and joking, trying to peep in, see the girl.

Probably good to do something about that.

He went to the door, opened it, and stepped outside. "Whoo-eee!" one of them yelped at him. "You havin' fun in thar, Dep?" The fellow was a short, broad-shouldered man in a dirty shirt and dented derby hat. A common laborer and likely no more of that than he could help.

Link crooked a finger at him, and the man stepped forward, grinning, possibly expecting some jape or other. When he was close enough, Link smiled at him, leaned in, and kicked him in the stones.

The man was strong, and tough enough. He stayed on his feet, and tried to keep standing straight, maybe with some notion of making a fight of it. But the pain gradually drew him down, made him begin to bend over. Link stepped into him again, and kicked him as hard as he could in the chest. His boot-toe jarred hard against the bones in the man's chest; it hurt Link's ankle a little. No one in the crowd was making any noise now. The fellow staggered away, trying to catch his breath.

Link kicked him again, in the back of his knee, and the man fell onto the boardwalk on his hands and knees. Link walked around to the man's side, and kicked him once more, in the side of the head. The fellow groaned in pain, and fell flat. He was crying, and trying to protect his head with his hands.

People were standing way back, now.

"Listen," Link said to them, raising his voice so all of them could hear him. "I'd rather not have you people making a fuss out here in the street. I think it would be better if you all went on about your business."

And damned if that crowd didn't just drift away.

It seemed to Link that the law business wasn't as tough as had been made out.

He stood outside the jail, watching the hurt man crawling down the walk; nobody had stopped to help the poor fellow. Then, Link went back inside the jail. The girl was quiet, cursed out. He walked into the other cell, stretched out on the hard, narrow bunk, tilted his Stetson brim down over his eyes, and started to drift off to sleep.

The ache in his side eased a little as he lay there. Link felt tired, but not too bad, despite that trouble with the drovers and the scramble out of the boardwalk. God knew he'd felt like dying this morning. Strange how getting some years on a man could cut at him. Man could rifle-fight some drovers, could kick a fellow down on the street, but put that same man to walking hard, carrying a heavy load, and it took but those years and a half-healed gunshot wound to put him in a faint.

Strange about those years, what they took from a man. Wasn't fair, of course. A few damn years . . . just the sun wheeling around, seasons changing. But those years struck at a man more surely than a knife. They cut at him, and wore him down.

Not fair. One of the big "not-fairs." And he could see how a man—or a woman, even more—could brood about that. Stare in mirrors, and get mad as hell about it.

Not likely to be Frank Leslie's problem for too much

longer. Not unless he started to sidestep trouble a little quicker than he had so far. Not much use changing a name, if you don't change your ways as well. One of these days, he was going to go to shoot a man and that man was going to shoot the shit right out of him instead. One of these days, he was going to try and whip the tar out of some loafer, and end up beat to a frazzle himself.

There were plenty of men around, be happy to do a quicker job than the years would ever do, on Buckskin Frank Leslie.

No . . . not much use worrying over old age. Unlikely ever to reach it.

He settled into the bunk, and felt his muscles easing. Probably hadn't had to kick that fellow that last time, make him cry like that. Not right for a man to get pleasure out of beating a fellow that way. Something empty in a man if he has to fill it with beating people so severely. Killing them . . .

Link slept.

He dreamed he was talking with the stable girl . . . Jean. And in the dream she was not stupid, not half-witted and dumb. In the dream, they were sitting in the parlor of a nice house in some big city; he could hear carriages going by out in the street—a cobblestone street, it sounded like.

The girl was like a lady, sitting up on a horsehair sofa with lace along the back, pouring cups of tea from a silver service. She and Link were talking about a horse race in Saratoga, New York—which made Link, in the dream, think the city they were in was New York City. As they talked, he tried to lean over a little bit, to look out through the curtains to see if the city was New York. "What in the world are you doing, Mister Leslie?" the stable girl said, just like a lady.

"What are you looking for out of my father's window?"

Link didn't know how to tell her he didn't know what city they were in, so he just made a joke about tea parties with beautiful girls making him nervous, and the stable girl laughed. She looked very pretty in her white dress; her hair was gathered up on her head in the way that young married ladies wore their hair, and he could faintly smell a trace of lemon vergena drifting from her when she leaned forward on the sofa to pour more tea.

He saw a plate of cakes beside the tray. They had sugar dusted over them, but he decided not to ask for one. If she offered, though, he thought he might take two, hold one on his napkin there on his knee while he was eating the other one. She looked very thin, for a lady, but she was a pretty girl. Married, he supposed.

They talked about the race, about the weather in Saratoga; they talked about the way the sports and gamblers were spoiling the town. It had been so beautiful, so carefully kept.

Link hoped she wasn't going to ask him which horse had won the damn race. *Bonnie Ben*, he thought. *Bonnie* something . . . "Would you care for a cake, Mister Leslie?" she said. He forgot about having two, and reached out and took the one. He saw that her hand was thin, and dirty, and worn, with broken nails. Her wrist, though, was white, and delicate as it could be. It ran up into the foamy white of the lace of her sleeve.

Link let his napkin slide off his lap, and, bending to get it back, looked under the table at her ankles. Her thin, dirty feet were bare, and he could see her legs above her ankles. They were scratched and dirty, and bruised up the shins. As he watched, he saw a thin run of dark blood slide down her calf, just a few drops

147

running down her leg, and he smelled the rotted salt-smell of spoiled blood.

He sat right up, with his napkin on his knee—he'd lost the cake. She smiled at him across the tea table, a girl, a lady in white, and said, "What did you see under my father's table, Mister Leslie? Did you see a secret?"

"No," he said, "I dropped my napkin."

She smiled. "I think you saw my secret," she said. "You see, I bleed from the place between my legs—where I have strange hair? I bleed from there, and I've not been able to ask anyone why . . . It is . . . too private."

Something was knocking on the wall . . .

Link woke . . . half-woke, and thought about where he was. It seemed less likely than having tea with the girl, and he supposed for a moment that that was the truth, and this was a dream.

The coaching girl was knocking on the wall, cursing.

"Say, you meaching son-of-a-bitch! Let me out of this or you'll God-damn well regret it!"

Pounding on the cell wall, or kicking it. Kicking it, more likely than not. Sounded like a kick.

Link shook the last of the dream out of his head, swung his boots to the floor, and stood up. Through the small office, he could see evening sunlight, soft gold against the dusty windows. Time for supper. Time to get supper for his prisoner, too, or let her go. Been enough fuss over a ducking, as it was. *His prisoner.* That was a laugh, and then some.

When he went out into the office, she must have heard him, because she began pounding on her cell door, or kicking it. And kept up the cursing and threats. Sounded tough as blazes.

Link unbarred her cell door, opened it and caught

her with her high-button shoe swung back for another
kick.

"You can stop that noise, right now," he said, "if
you want out of here."

"You kiss my butt," she said, coarse as a barrelhouse
whore. But she blushed after she said it. Maybe not as
tough as blazes, then. Maybe just a plump little pigeon
playing Jane Canary.

"You be still, now," Link said, "and I'll bring you
some supper, and let you go in the morning." When it
looked like she intended to start in cursing and threat-
ening again, he added, "Only a tenderfoot acts
tougher than he is." And she shut up.

No one paid much heed to him on his way over to
the Rose for supper. He'd thought of trying another
chow-pot, but none that he'd seen looked worth it.
The old Chinaman was likely the best cook in town,
judging from the suppertime crowd in his kitchen.

A few people looked at him out of the corner of their
eyes as he walked, but they didn't stare. They didn't
wish him a good evening, either. Appeared to be of
two minds about the new law in town—longed for old
Swazee to be up and about, probably. Well, Link was
damn well of two minds, too. And one mind said he
was making a fine fool of himself with this cheap
deputy's badge. It might give him an edge with the
Coes; then after all, it might not. Back-shot dead as a
damned copper-carrier . . . A rotten way to go.

The Rose was packed when he walked through the
batwing doors, full of drovers, yard-workers, and
lumberyard loafers. One of those men was standing at
the end of the bar with a beer mug in his hand and an
odd bandage plastered to his nose. By the bandage,
Link recognized one of the men from the stable loft.
The fellow seemed none the worse for wear except for
a mite shorter nose than was common. He appeared

jolly enough, joking and swigging at his beer. Link looked for a red-headed man near the fellow; that was a man who might carry a grudge for being beaten. He looked, but saw no red-headed man. Might have gotten off Scot free on that jape. He was surer of that when he saw himself pointed out by someone in that bunch—for the gunfight, or the badge—and could see that bandage-nose made nothing special of him. The light in that loft had been just poor enough . . .

Link pushed through the crowd—he didn't have to push hard—reached the bar, and called to a fat Mex-looking man tending the mahogany. He ordered a short beer and whiskey-shot, ignored the space men had made on each side of him, and drank the whiskey down, and then the beer, without wasting much time about it. The Mex-looking fellow seemed to know his business at serving drinks. He was slow, but he got his orders straight. Somewhere, MacDuff had picked up an old man with a hollow left eye-socket to help out back there. He was working the other end of the wood, having some trouble keeping up, too, it looked like.

Link got tired of having so much clear space around him. He turned to a man down the bar on his right, a tall man dressed like a workman, but with a gentleman's side-whiskers, sandy colored.

"Been a nice, warm day," Link said to him. "Pleasant change."

"Yes, sir, it has," the man said, raising his voice a little over the noise of the crowd. He was down the bar a yard, at least. "It sure has, at that."

"Be pleased to buy you a drink," Link said, feeling flush, with twenty-five dollars of the town's money in his trouser pocket, an advance on a deputy's pay. Charmian must have thought he'd feel obliged not to run once he'd taken their money. The old trap hadn't missed much of her bet, that was sure.

"Now, I'm obliged for the offer, but I don't have the time to accept it," Side-whiskers said. "If you'd give me a rained-out check, I'd certainly appreciate it." And he finished his drink with a rush, pushed off from the bar, and was gone.

The respect a man earned with killings was a piss-poor sort. The sort you'd rather not have at all.

"Say now, Deputy, damn your eyes! Are you scarin' all my customers away, god-damn you?!"

"Have a beer with me, MacDuff."

"Cash drawer money, is it?"

"Badge money, Scotchman."

"Then I'll buy my own," MacDuff said. "I'm used to the coppers cadging off me; the contrary makes me nervous. You staying the night?" He waved to his new bartender, signalling with his fist for a mug of beer.

"No, I'll sleep in the jail."

"It's where you belong; not a doubt of that," MacDuff said. "I suppose you'll be wanting George to carry your traps over for you?"

"Tomorrow's soon enough," Link said. "I'd appreciate it. I damn sure seem a poor hand at lugging."

"It's the age coming on you," MacDuff said, with some satisfaction, and drank half his beer. "What do you think of this new barminder of mine? He's not the beer-puller you are, but then he's not so quick at the drawer, either."

"He's fair enough," Link said, comforted in some way by the conversation, enjoying the ease of it. "Slow."

"Yes, he's slow—it's the latin blood, I expect. Sees no need to hurry the whiskey down the throats of fools." MacDuff chewed his mustache for a moment, looking at Link out of the corner of his eye. "No need," he said, "no need to stay in the Creek unless you care

151

to, for all the Coe drovers . . ."

Link looked at him.

"I . . . that is, some of us . . . well, we could pack you in a goods wagon, and freight you out to Boise free and clear and not a Coe the wiser about it either, the dirty dogs."

Link thought about it, and thought as well of the Coe riders riding laughing around a freight wagon, poking through the load with the muzzles of their Winchesters. He could see it very clearly. Could hear them laughing. Of course, he might go out of town on the stage, dressed as a woman. Maybe with a blue poke bonnet on his head. Maybe beg that big-mouth coaching girl to drive him.

"No," he said. And MacDuff looked away form him.

MacDuff finished his beer, and put the mug carefully back on the bar. Then he said, without looking at Link, "A Rocking-D cowpoker was in here drunk not an hour ago. He spilled that Billy Coe and Reed Coe are home. Rode into the ranch this afternoon, damn them. They must have killed horses getting back so soon. Anse Coe had a telegraph wire sent to them from Bitternut, sure as hell."

"Sooner or later," Link said. "It makes no difference." He felt just as pleased it would soon be over.

"So you say," MacDuff said. "So you say, you damn fool. They've brought a man with them. What do you think of that?" He toyed with the empty beer mug. "Trust that pack to eucre their bet!"

"Who's this fellow?" Link said. He could see that MacDuff knew him, at least by reputation.

"Name's Busey," MacDuff said. "Henry Busey."

Link had heard of the man—a woman killer, he'd heard, came from the Oregon territory. Supposed to

152

be a fine hand with a pistol, too, but that was said of any bad man.

"I've heard of him."

"You have, huh?" MacDuff said. "You're heard of him, have you? Have you heard he took a woman and her daughter off a ranch in Colorado while the men were on roundup? Took those women out into the woods and outraged the both of them, then tied them to a tree, piled brush around them, and burned them both alive." He signalled his Mex bartender for a fresh beer. "Heard of that, did you?"

"Something of that sort," Link said. "Something about him killing women."

"Oh, he murders girls, all right, but he's not so slow when it comes to killing men, either. The rancher whose women he'd taken? Well, that man and six good hands took after Busey . . . chased that bastard for more than a month. Then they caught him."

MacDuff got his beer, and swigged from it and whiped foam from his mustache. "Two of the hands got out of that fight alive. Said Busey'd drawn them into badlands, run 'em ragged. Then one night, deep into dark, he came creeping into camp with a long-blade Spanish sticker, and damned if he hadn't gone to those sleeping men, one by one, and pushed that blade down into an eye, all the way down into their brain-jelly. And not a single sound did he make, doing it." MacDuff took another swallow of beer. "Did for the rancher and three hands that way. The night guard came in and caught him at it, and Busey started shootin', laughing fit to beat a band while he did it, too. Killed another of the drovers, killed him and wounded another. That man, and the last, just took off runnin'—no horses under them or nothin'. Just took off runnin'. Walked into a town seven days later—been hikin' wounded and barefoot in the chapperal all that time."

"Fellow sounds mad," Link said.

"Mad as a dog gone foamin' and chewing its tongue. But you'd never know it to talk to him."

"You know him?"

"I met him in Fort James," MacDuff said lowering his voice. "A fellow named Pomfret and me had a hotel there. This Busey used to rent a room sometimes. We didn't want to rent to him. Fact is, we were scared not to. Yet to meet the man, you wouldn't think he was wrong at all. Big man, fancy dresser—always wearing some kind of flash vest, striped or something. Great talker, Busey." MacDuff tilted his head way back and downed his beer to the bottom of the mug. "Well, one fine night, I heard a hell of a racket up on the second floor, yelling . . . laughin'. I figured it was just drunk horse-play. Well, in the mornin' this Flathead girl went up there to Busey's room to clean, you know? Went up there and let out the most God-awful yell you ever heard. The most God-awful sound. Busey'd murdered a woman up there. A respectable woman, too, sister of the dentist in town. That madman had cut her open, pulled her insides right out of her, and damned if he didn't hang her with her own insides."

"And the town put up with that?" said Link.

MacDuff laughed and shook his head. "They damn surely did," he said, "because when they ran to the marshal's office to get a posse up, they found out Busey'd been a long step ahead of them. That mad son-of-a-bitch had gone in there the night before—must have been just before he got the woman up to his room —and why the hell she went up there, I'll never know, because she was a decent woman; she was a widow, had a kid. But Busey must have planned it all. When

Palmer and the rest of those men went to the marshal's office, they found him deader than a doornail. Busey had beat that man's head in like you'd stomp on a tin cup."

"So the town stepped back."

"Stepped way to hell back! And I didn't blame them, and I don't blame them now. Busey rode out that afternoon, rode out at a walk, and swung down for a drink at the Twobit before he left. Full of jokes and good humor, too. Always full of jokes . . ."

"Sounds a deadly fellow, if you're a woman or unwary," Link said. "And still free of the law, and a friend of the Coes?"

"From what I hear," MacDuff said, lowering his voice a little more, "he plays parts like a stage actor and sticks to the high lonesome more often than not. But they'll get him one day—they don't forget it if you smash a lawman like a damn bug! They'll bring him in to a judge one day and they'll hang him like a salt-ham, and good riddance!"

From this, Link thought that perhaps MacDuff had not thought the yelling upstairs in his hotel had been just drunken funning. Had known the woman to be in desperate trouble, and had been afraid to do anything about it. Hard. Hard to blame a fellow who was no particular fighting man for not stepping upstairs to face a bad man like Busey. It appeared likely, though, that MacDuff blamed himself over it.

"Let's get out of this," MacDuff said, nodding at the crowd thick and noisy around them. Thick, but still leaving room at Link's elbow. MacDuff lead the way through the customers, exchanging a word here and there, and on up the balcony stairs. At the top of the steps he turned to Link.

"Now, you listen to me, Mister Gunman," he said. "I've seen you shoot in a barroom fight and you're

155

good at it. You may be better with a revolver than Busey; I don't know. You may be a better shot than Reed Coe, too, though I doubt it. And I'm not even talking about Billy Coe, who's as cruel as a bird-snake. What I'm saying is that neither you, nor any other man alive is fierce enough or quick enough to face both those men—and I'm not even including Billy!"

Link reached out and touched MacDuff on the shoulder. "You've been a good friend, Mac," he said. "But I—"

"Don't you tell me you don't have a choice! Any damn fool has the choice to run! I say we can get you out of this . . ."

"I don't want out of it," Link said. And was surprised to find that it was so.

MacDuff pushed Link's hand away from his shoulder. "Do you want to die, then?" he said.

Link started to say that he didn't know, then stopped. It was too personal a thing to say. It surprised him even to think of that sort of thing.

MacDuff stood looking at him, waiting for him to answer. When Link said nothing, MacDuff blew through his mustaches like an exasperated horse.

"You're a fool, Mister, and I'll have nothing more to do with you!" He turned away and walked down the hall to his office door. Then he turned to look back. "George'll take your goods over in the morning," he said, and added, "Good luck, and God help you" as he opened his door, went in, and closed it behind him.

One of the very few advantages that Link had found in being habitually in desperate fights was the sometimes sharp understanding it had given him of certain ways that people held to. MacDuff now, he understood very well. The man was a decent fellow and a friend. But he wanted Link to run, as if Link's running might make his own shyness easier to bear. But how many men, some quite strong and accustomed to arms, would have climbed the rough-sawn steps of that log walled hotel in Fort James to stop Henry Busey from doing what he was engaged in doing?

Not many. Not many.

So Link regarded MacDuff as still a friend, and didn't blame him for adding to his concern a wish that Link would hide in a wagon and be sneaked at night out of Colt Creek.

Link went back down the stairs and made his way through the crowd and noise, and some men who were dancing buck-and-wings with the two fat girls beside the piano. It was the first time Link had seen somebody playing the piano, a store clerk in a yellow-checked jacket, with oil in his hair. Link went down the side corridor to the kitchen, and found the place much the same as it had been the last time he was there. The old Chinaman presided at his big black range, the long table packed with yard men and drovers, all stuffing themselves like stray dogs. The huge man who'd been in the kitchen before was there again, eating a meal fit for three big men. The kitchen was hazy with cook-smoke, hot, and full of the smell of food, wool, leather, whiskey and sweat.

That little sleep in the cell had helped. Link felt well. Hungry. He thought that he didn't feel like a man who wanted to die.

Some of the men around the table nodded to Link in a friendly way. Some eyes lingered on the badge. Link supposed there was considerable betting going on about this and that: whether the Coes would come in and kill him tonight, or tomorrow, or the day after. Whether he'd take one with him—another one, that is, not counting the deceased fat Charley Coe. Bets of all kinds were made on situations like this. Link had done his share of wagering too, in other days. Won a

157

few, lost a few.

The old Chinaman took a serving spoon out of one of his pots, and waved to Link with it. "You want supper, Marshal?" His tied-up beard waggled as he talked.

"I do—and one for road, for my prisoner." Felt damn odd to be saying something of that sort: "For my prisoner." *Be glad when this charade-game is over.*

Two men made room for him at the end of the table, and the Chinaman came over, grinning, with a plate for him. The old man seemed to think Link was acting out a stage-play for his amusement and it was hard to see how that wasn't so. The huge man, sitting several places down, began picking up platters and passing them down: root-cellar stuff, first. Boiled onions, mashed potatoes, sweet potatoes baked with honey, and buttered carrots. Then, platters of meat—a heap of thick, smoking pork chops, a platter of pan-cooked chicken, and a third piled with slices of salt-ham and cooked apple. Link took all that his plate would bear, and then stacked chunks of hot corn bread on top, in a sort of Leaning Tower arrangement—reminded him of a stereopticon of that building he had seen.

A pitcher of iced buttermilk, or a pitcher of cold beer from the bar were the offered beverages. Link poured himself a tall glass of buttermilk, took a deep drink of it, and dug into his food.

Except for the sounds of eating, and the clink and clatter of knives and forks against the chinaware, it became a quiet table. After a few minutes, when the present portions were gone, men called for more food and were passed it and fell to eating again. Link found it very restful.

CHAPTER 11

LINK WAS laughing when he unlocked the door to the marshal's office. He had a lunch pail for the coaching girl with her supper in it, but the pail was a mite dented.

He'd just had another try at enforcing the law.

Two drunks, common loafers by the look of them, had been hollering and hoorahing under some whore's window on Pierson Street, Link, heading back to the office, had come upon them, flashed his new badge, and told them to shut up and get home. One of them, a bald-headed fellow, had swaggered and said to hell with you. Link hated hitting people with his revolver; it was bad for the weapon. He'd known drovers who'd swat horses between the ears with the barrels of their .45's to stop them bucking and later were puzzled that the pieces didn't shoot true to target.

He swung the lunch pail on the fellow instead and it had made a satisfying clang against his head. The loafer had collapsed into his friend's arms, weeping and wobble-legged, and Link had advised them again to hush their fuss and get home. When they were on their way, he'd continued on his, his duty done for the night, he hoped. The Coes had gone a fair way toward taming Colt Creek to their own advantage, and Link was glad enough of that. He'd had no notion, in taking the badge for a few days, to play Bill Tilghman with it, and spend his nights dealing with drunken drovers and pistol-mad hoodlums. The badge was to his purpose, not the town's.

He pushed open the office door and was greeted by an angry shout from out of the dark. His prisoner was apparently finding the time heavy on her hands.

"Hold your horses," Link said. "Be quiet in there—I've got your supper for you." He didn't add that the supper was liable to be somewhat jumbled from hitting the loafer's head.

"You let me out of here, you dirty son-of-a-bitch!"

Link was getting tired of that bad mouth on her. He lit a kerosene lantern on the marshal's desk, and by the dim yellow light went over and unbarred her door.

The girl was huddled back on the cell cot, looking in the faint lantern light like a small rumpled, round-faced cat. Her grey eyes glinted in the light.

"Keep quiet now, and come out here and eat your supper."

Standing at the doorway to the little cell, Link could smell the cheap perfume she was wearing—she smelled enough like a whore, that was for sure—and the faint, acrid smell of her piss. She'd used the slop bucket.

"Come on. Come on out here and eat."

She got up then, and came sidling out into the lantern light. She saw the lunch pail on the table and edged around the table to it. Then, keeping an eye on Link, she pulled one of the old cane-bottom chairs up to the table, sat down, and went right to work prying at the lunch pail lid.

Dammit—he'd forgotten to bring eating utensils. Couldn't see her eating her meal with her fingers. Link was looking around the shadowy office for something that might serve, when she wrenched the lid off the pail and immediately had something to say.

"What in the world is this cowshit? What happened to it? It's all messed up!"

"It hit something," Link said, and was pleased to see her dig a spoon out of the pail. It seemed to be covered with wet cornbread.

"Hit something?" She gave him an angry look. "This is a damn mess—and I'll be double God-damned if I'll eat it!"

"Suit yourself," Link said. "But you're not getting out of here until tomorrow, whatever. So—I'm sorry it's mixed up like that—even so, you better try and eat it, because I'm sure not walking back to get you another supper."

"Cow shit," she said, and bent her head and spit down into the pail. "Now *you* eat it, Deputy!"

Link felt a flush mounting in his face, but he held his temper, pulled up another chair, and sat down across from her. "What's your name, Miss?" he said, like a very proper City Marshal.

"Nancy Plum," the girl said, and it occured to Link that she was well named, at that, with her round cheeks and sturdy figure. She looked something like a ripe plum . . . "But they call me 'Drivin' Nan,' " she added, with some satisfaction. "No man in this town can run a four-horse team better than me and most of them a hell of a lot worse!"

"How old are you, Nancy?" It seemed to him she was considerably younger than her talk. Nineteen, twenty would be his guess.

"None of your damned business," she said, and shoved the lunch pail over the table to him. "Why don't you eat that shit yourself," she said, "and let me the hell out of here. I got a stage to load and way-bill

161

and I can't do it sitting on my hindmost in the clink!"

"You just drive that rig or do you have an owning interest?" Link said.

"I have a damn good interest: thirty-five percent, bought and paid for." She pushed her chair back, and stood up. "How's about I give you a ten-dollar gold piece to let me out? I got business to do and I never saw a deputy turn down a yellow-bit."

Link saw that he had been right. She was one of those girls who'd come far West to shake out of petticoats. Sounded like Missouri or Kansas by her flat way of talking. Probably had some money left her by an aunt, or her Granny, and she'd kissed the farm goodbye and come out here to live free as a man—or nearly so. Her bit of money had saved her from playing frig-sister in a house, had bought her into that little freight fit-out. No question that she'd learned to drive; she did handle a team better than most men. Good hand with a whip, too.

And Link saw that she was frightened of jail. There was no way-billing she had to do tonight; she just didn't care to be locked up. It frightened her. This hard-case "Drivin' Nan" looked to have never seen the inside of a jail before in her life. He might as well let her go, at that. She'd shied off his hat and he'd dumped her. She'd hit him and he'd locked her up for a while. No need to hold her scared the whole night.

"Here," she said, and tossed the ten-dollar piece down on the table. "Bite down on that, put it in your pocket, and let me out, Tin-badge. It's more gelt than you'll see honest in a week." And she brushed by him, on her way to the office door and out.

Link, annoyed, stood up and reached to stop her. That tongue of hers had about earned her a night in jail!

Reached for her—and quick as a cat she jumped in

behind him, fumbled at his waist and got her hand on the grip of the Bisley Colt's. Link slammed his hand down on hers to keep her from drawing the piece and turned against her as fast as he could. She was thrown against the wall, lost her hold on the revolver grip and came back at him with a yell, swinging her small fists like a man.

Link swung to hit her as she came in on him and caught himself just in time to open his fist before it struck her. The flat of his hand hit her across the side of the face, knocked her head sharply to the side so that spit came flying from her open mouth, hurled her back into the wall.

She slid down to the floor, dazed, her eyelids fluttering, and Link leaned down, gripped her under the armpits, lifted her up, and carried her, her high-button boots dangling off the floor, into her cell.

Little Miss Calamity Jane had God-damned well earned her night in jail. Maybe a week!

She came fully awake as he toted her in, started to put her down on the cot. "Ohh, nooo . . ." It built to a scream. "*Ahh, Noooo . . .!*" It was loud enough to wake the dead.

Link tossed her down on the cot, leaned over her, and clamped his hand down over her mouth. He felt her teeth work against his palm, and cupped it so she couldn't get a fair bite on him.

"You shut your mouth." Spoken right into her ear, so she couldn't miss it. It did no good. She thrashed and kicked against him as if he intended murder, reached up to strike at his face with her nails, and drew a frantic breath in through her nose to howl the louder when she could.

If he'd a riding crop handy, he could have smartened her into silence double quick. As it was, Link found himself hanging on to this sturdy little

163

wildcat, trying to keep from smothering her, and at the same time prevent her from screaming half the town awake and on down to the jail to see an outrage. It was such an odd pickle that he began to laugh, still wrestling with her tooth and nail, laugh hard enough so that once she almost squirmed away from him.

But enough was enough. The girl was struggling like a mad thing, and was bound to be hurt if it continued. Link had never cared for the forcible taming of decent girls into whores, though he'd not been too nice to recruit the doves, once soiled. A man can't run two Fort Gaither parlor houses and be too nice about it. What the gay life taught you, you never forgot. It was the school of schools.

Keeping the palm of his hand over the girl's mouth, he stretched his thumb and index finger up a bit, and pinched her nostrils shut. "Burking" it was called, after some Scotch fellow.

Her air cut off, she thrashed and struck at him hysterically, but not for long. She soon began to falter, hitting out at him, to kick and buck in slow, useless, spasmodic ways. Her eyes, grey as rain, huge, terrified, stared up at him as she writhed under his hands. She heaved up as he bent over her, and Link felt the soft cushions of her breasts against him. She twisted, convulsed, trying to breathe, her skirts riding high on round white thighs. Link smelled her sweat mingling with her perfume and the faint gluey smell of her privates.

His cock had stiffened in his trousers. Not fair. Not fair to take advantage of her . . .

Shit. Tomorrow he might be shot to rags, and if not tomorrow, then soon enough. He'd intended to let her go—would have, if she hadn't played tough, trying for the revolver.

He took his hand off her face, listened for a

moment, and heard the desperate shuddering breath she drew. He walked out into the office, went to the door, and opened it. There were some people in the dark street, a group of drovers across the way, stomping down the boardwalk, drunk, some men loading a wagon further down. No one looked to be coming to a lady's rescue, having heard screams. Dark streets; you had to strain your eyes to see a thing. At least they should have some oil lanterns strung on poles. Two or three to a block shouldn't cost the town more than it could afford. As it was, old Swazee must have had his hands full with just the petty theives alone. It would take a round half dozen deputies with baseball bats in their hands walking the town at night to keep a real peace with no light at all falling on the streets. Link supposed that honest citizens stayed on Main at night or stayed home.

He closed the office door and locked it, went over to the table to blow out the lamp, then changed his mind, picked it up, and carried it back into her cell.

The Driving Girl lay huddled on the cot, her legs drawn up under her skirts. She stared into the lantern light, her eyes big, her face as pale as paper.

"Leave me alone," she said. "Please . . ." She sounded hoarse, and was speaking softly. No more playing the hard-case.

"I'll trouble you a little," Link said. "Then, if you don't like it, I'll stop." He set the lantern on the floor, and began to unbutton his shirt.

"Please don't do anything," she said, and pressed back harder against the wall.

Link leaned against the door frame for support while he pulled off his boots and socks. He saw her eyes gleaming in the golden lantern light. She was staring at him.

He unbuckled his gunbelt, walked over to the cot,

165

bent, and set the holstered weapon on the floor, under the cot's edge. Too far under for her to reach without crawling down there after it. He doubted she'd be searching his boots, and so come upon the Arkansas toothpick.

She had shrunk back when he came close to her, but Link paid her no more mind while he shucked out of his trousers and long johns. Then he turned to her.

She'd buried her face in her arms, lay curled up on the dirty brown blanket. She had pretty hair, dark and shining, all tangled now, with her struggling. He reached down and stroked it, trying to gentle her, as he would a frightened horse.

She mumbled something, and Link said, "What?"

"I said," she said into her folded arms, her voice shaking, "If you . . . if you hurt me . . . my friends will kill you." She caught her breath, and he could tell she was weeping. "They'll . . . they'll kill you."

"No, they won't," Link said, and he sat down on the cot, naked. His cock was straining up so hard it was hurting him, but he held himself back, to be as gentle with her as he could, getting what he was going to get. "No, they won't because they're never going to hear about it. Nobody is. This is going to be between you and me."

She sat up suddenly, and her face was tear-streaked, contorted with crying. "Oh, *please* don't . . . *please don't do anything!*" Her voice was rising, and Link leaned over and slapped her gently across the face, not hard enough to hurt her. Then she was quiet. She sat staring at him, breathing as if she'd been running somewhere. She looked at his cock.

"Have you seen a man's cock before?" Link said to her. "I don't think that you have." He leaned over and put his arm around her. She was shivering like an

166

aspen in autumn, high up, on the Divide. "Well, it's all for you, Nancy," he said. "You can touch it . . . play with it. You can kiss it, if you want."

"Oh, please . . . Mister . . ."

Link shook her a little. "I've heard enough of that," he said. "Hell, you're no child—you're a grown-up woman, and one with more guts than most, to come out here from your home and make your way." He reached around to the bodice of her dress with his free hand, and found the row of little buttons there, found the top one, and after a try, managed to undo it. They were little round buttons, and difficult to get loose, but he went down the row, and undid them one by one.

Once, she put up a small cold hand there to try and stop him, but he pushed it roughly away, and then she sat quietly and didn't try to stop him again.

"You come all this way," Link said. "All the way out here, like a kid playing a game. Damn if I don't think you read old Ned Buntline . . . you probably have . . . and then come out here, and try living wild and free . . ." He felt tears on his hand, where he was undoing the buttons on the bodice of her dress.

He bent closer to her, and spoke softly in her ear. "But I think you wanted other things. I smelled you, when we were tussling—smelled what's between your pretty legs . . . and that, what's between your legs . . . it wants something . . ." He opened the last button, slid his hand under the dress material, and onto her breasts covered with soft cotton.

"Don't do that," she said, speaking so softly that he barely heard her. She put up her hands to try and close the front of her dress, but he pushed them aside and began to stroke and knead her breasts through the cotton shift. Her breasts were big, weighty as soft

167

melons in his hand. He stroked and squeezed them gently, molding the cloth to them, cupping them in his hand. He looked at her face in the lamplight, and saw that her eyes were tight shut, like a child's, frightened of what it might see. After a moment, searching, his fingers found her nipples, small and soft for such heavy breasts. He pinched them gently.

"Stop it!" She turned and hit out at him, trying to hit his hands, keep them away from her. Link caught her wrists, held them, then shifted his grip so that he held both of them in one hand.

"Leave me *alone!*" She was almost yelling. Link tightened his grip on her wrists until she gasped with pain.

"You be still for a while," he said, found the strings tying her shift closed, and pulled them loose. She tried to wrench away from him then, but he held her wrists hard and tugged her shift open. He saw her naked breasts shining white in the lantern light, saw the faint pink circles, the small, soft nipples. He could hear her weeping softly.

Link let go of her wrists, put his hands on the shoulders of her dress, and began to pull her open dress and shift down off her shoulders, down her upper arms. He tugged her arms free, first the left, then the right.

Her big breasts, gleaming white, swung and shook as he pulled the bodice down, freeing them. When the girl was naked to the waist, Link sat back for a moment, looking at her.

She sat, her head bowed, trembling a little. He put his arm around her, holding her to him. "Don't be scared, Sis," he said. He stroked her bare breasts gently, just touching her with his fingertips. "All this was meant for something, you know—something beside playing tough." He cupped one of her breasts in his hand, and squeezed it. "This soft titty isn't tough. It's soft as cream."

He bent over and put his mouth to the delicate nipple, and began to lick it. He felt her stiffen, and try to strain away, but he kept his arm around her, held her close, and, nuzzling into her breast like a hungry baby, began to suck at her nipple, tugging gently at the soft flesh. He did this for a while, then gradually opened his mouth wider, taking more of her breast into his mouth, sucking, biting lightly at the swelling nipple.

She moved restlessly in his arms, and said something. Link sat up, still holding her breast cupped in his hand. The nipple, protruding now, and dark red in the lantern light, was glistening with saliva.

"That feel good? Hmnn?" She didn't say anything; Link saw she was looking down at herself, at her naked breasts. "Didn't any boy ever get you alone, and do that to you—feel your pretty titties and play with you?" He put his hand on her other breast, and shook it gently, watched the white, shining flesh wobble. "You're a beautiful woman."

She stirred, trying to free her hands, but he held her wrists firmly, trying not to hold so hard as to hurt her. Then, when she quieted, he bent to her other breast and began as he had before, to gently lick and suck at her, finally to nuzzle and suck as strongly at her as a hungry baby, tugging and lightly biting at her nipple, sucking it strongly, sucking hard, drawing the soft, small nipple up, and firmer, until it was swollen hard.

She began to lean against him. To push a little against his insistent mouth. He could feel her heart pounding through the wet flesh against his lips.

He sat up suddenly, and she sagged against him. He let go of her wrists and gripped her breasts with both hands, kneading them, squeezing them so hard that

169

she moaned. He rolled the stiff nipples between his thumbs and forefingers, pinching them so sharply that she drew in her breath with the pain. She put her hands on his forearms for a moment, as if she could make him stop what he was doing. But she didn't try. Her hands lay on his arms, gripped them lightly, only tightening when he hurt her.

"I wish you'd stop it," she said, almost whispering. "Please."

Link let go her breasts, and reached out and hugged her to him, feeling those soft, damp, bruised teats against his chest. He put a hand in her hair, pulled her head slightly back so that her face was turned up to him, and gently kissed her. Her lips were soft, and she held them closed like a little girl, kissing.

Link hugged her so hard that she grunted, and gasped for breath; when her mouth opened under his he seized on it as if it were a Mexican mango-fruit, but gently at it, and sucked and drank its juices as if he'd been dying of thirst. She struggled for a moment, twisting in his arms, then, slowly, first a little, then more, she relaxed for him, letting her mouth go slack so that his tongue could drive fully into her, so that he could lick her teeth, the smooth wet insides of her lips, could find her tongue and tease it, and suck on it.

She groaned into his mouth, and let him do what he wanted.

Link kissed her until he felt her chest heave for air, and then a little longer. He gripped her shoulders, and pushed her down until she lay on the rumpled brown blanket.

Even as she lay flat, her round breasts sagged only slightly to each side. She stared up at him through the soft tangle of her hair, with a dulled, dreamy look, as though she'd smoked a Frisco pipe. She didn't move when he took her hand and put it on his cock, letting

170

her feel the hardness and the heat there. She gripped it firmly and turned her head to look at what she was doing.

"You like that?"

She didn't answer; just lay breathing quickly, looking at it, stiff and swollen in the grip of her small hand. A little moisture had appeared at the tip, and Link touched his finger to it, and then smeared it lightly across her lips.

"Lick it," he said.

After a moment, slowly, she put out the tip of her tongue, and licked her lips.

Link reached down to the hem of her dress, and began to gather the folds of material up around her legs, slowly pushing them higher, up past the tops of her high-button boots, up over the smooth black silk stockings covering her sturdy, plump calves. He began to gently stroke her legs along the stockings' smoothness, gripping her soft calves, squeezing them as he had her breasts.

She muttered something, and put her hands down, trying to push his away, and Link stopped what he'd been doing, took one of her hands, held it to his mouth, and began to lick her palm, licking it as a cat would, in long, steady strokes.

After a while, he stopped, and began to stroke her legs again, squeezing the soft muscles until she murmured at the pain, then tickling her behind her knees, in the tender hollows there. And after that, gently, gently, slid his hands up and up along her thighs, kneading the muscles and soft flesh, tickling the sensitive skin through the smooth, shining silk.

Nancy Plum stirred restlessly on the narrow cot. Her legs shifted under his hands.

Above the black silk where ruffled garters circled her thighs, her skin shone like white gold in the lantern

171

light. The soft light seemed to shine through the flesh. Sturdy, round, and plump, with strong muscle just beneath the milky softness.

Link was pleased to see that this young adventuress in the Wild West hadn't adopted the Eastern custom among ladies lately of wearing some drawers or pantelettes under her skirt. He could smell her—and, as the tips of his fingers slid higher, smoothing the white flesh, he could feel the slighest touch of soft curls against them now and again.

He leaned up over her, and kissed her again gently. She took her hand off his cock, hesitated, then slowly reached up to put her arms around him. She hugged him awkwardly, her face flushed, hair tousled. When he put his face down to hers again, she kissed his cheek.

Link held her for a moment more, then pulled free to kiss the wet, swollen nipples of her breasts and slid further down to kneel between her legs. He stroked the silky backs of her knees, cupped a hand under each of them, and slowly lifted until the girl's legs were doubled, knees in the air, her high-button boots on the cot's blanket.

Then he put his hands on her, and slowly, steadily pulled her legs apart. When he felt a sudden resistance in her muscles, Link said, "Don't do that . . ." as he might have to a restive mare and kept up that steady pull until he felt a trembling slacking in her strength there. Her legs under his hands, slowly, slowly spraddled wide. Link saw the rising great tendon at the insides of her thighs, and he leaned forward, slid his hands down to the cool, plump rounds of her buttocks, lifted her, and in the same motion shoved the folds of her dress high up on her hips.

Then he sat back to look.

She lay panting and ashamed, her arms crossed over her face, hiding from the lantern light, her big breasts with their small swollen nipples shaking slightly with her breathing. Below the dark, gathered material of her dress's skirt, her round white thighs sprawled wide so that he could see everything.

She had a savage, dark little clump of curls where her thighs met, strained so wide she'd tugged slightly open the tender slit beneath the damp patch of hair. Link slid his hands down her thighs, dug his fingers into her, and gently pulled her wide open. The girl moaned into her folded arms when he did that, but she did nothing else.

Her small cunt had come open with a soft, sticky sound, and lay between his fingers like a half-healed wound, pink lipped, narrow, oily with fluid, and inside, wet, red, and deep. The hair straggled from it in little wisps, running down into the deep crack of her ass.

Link had known many men—many of them sports, too, cadets and pimps—who wouldn't touch a woman whose quim hadn't been fresh bathed and dabbed with French perfume as well, if she were expensive. Link had found all that pleasant enough, but, more often than not, unnecessary. He had no objection to a woman's ripe smells. He liked them, from the dark, salty smell of a woman's curse to the harsh fish-glue scent that cooked in a girl unwashed in hot weather.

That last was Nancy Plum's smell, sweeter to Link than any French perfume.

He bent down to kiss her there, and felt her stiffen as his lips touched the soft, damp little gash. He paid no attention, but leaned into her, held her thighs wide, his fingers digging into the white flesh, opened his mouth against her cunt as he had against her other

173

lips, and began to kiss her. Tenderly, easily, running the tip of his tongue along the slippery edges, sucking gently to get a little juice out of her.

The girl groaned as he worked on her, holding her thighs up and apart, opening her like a book, licking and sucking at the wet, swollen red split that lay spread open before him. He licked down the line of soaked dark curls below it, slid his hands down to thumb her ass cheeks apart, lifting her soft, round buttocks higher, bent his head to run his tongue on down to the small pleated button of her asshole, and, as she gasped and twisted in his hands, thrust his tongue deep into her.

Slowly, then, Link settled to his pleasure, using every old pimp's trick as he mouthed the girl's bottom from ass to cunt, finally slipping his tongue deeper and deeper into her kitty, probing, curling, lapping, sucking at her until he tasted a new taste on his tongue, oily, soft and sweet under the traces of girl sweat, and girl piss, and girl gash. This new stuff, light as gun-oil, had come welling from deep inside her. It was the oil to smooth the way to everything—to sooth the tearing of her maidenhead, as well. He'd touched the thin tissue with the tip of his tongue.

Nancy Plum was set to pay a due.

Link's cock was hurting him—it was time to use it. He gripped the girl's calves, spread them, and held them high. He rose against her on his knees, then let go one of her legs to hold his cock, and place the swollen tip of it against her gap, hunched forward, and thrust into her.

It drove in with a soft wet sound and Link felt the faint snap of her virginity just before the girl screamed, and smothered her scream with her own hands.

And he was in.

Link lay over her, propped up on stiffened arms, looking down into her face. She stared up at him, eyes wild, mouth open in astonishment at what was happening to her. Link moved his hips, pulling the length of his cock half out of her, and saw the exquisite sensation mirrored in her eyes. He slowly thrust in again, feeling the hot wet squeeze of her around him, slippery with juice and blood.

"Oh, don't . . ." she murmured to him. "Please don't do that to me . . ."

Then, he began to fuck her. Driving into her, thrusting in with all his strength—splitting her, riding all the way in to nudge the soft mouth of her womb as she lay spraddled, taking it all. She cried out again, then, as his cock slid deep into her. "You're hurting me! Oh . . . oh . . . You're *hurting* me . . ."

She tried to struggle, to wrestle against him, to push him off her, her breasts wobbling, her white arms writhing to shove him away, out of her. Link smelled the blood between them, and the sticky gravy of love and he rode her as she bucked just as, once, in the mountains to the west, he had broken to saddle the mares of a herd of Appaloosas, the beautiful little big-eyed mares that singlefooted through the hills like spotted ghosts.

Long gone, now. Gone and nearly forgotten.

After a little while . . . after Link had driven and driven into her and bent his head to catch her lips, and kissed her deep, and sucked her honey out . . . after his cock, red, and hard as oak, had played in and out, and in and out of her swollen, soaking cunt, drawing the inflamed little lips out with it then driving them back in an oily wet tangle of red meat and plastered hair . . after a little while of this, the girl began to grunt, deep, desperate, striving sounds as if she were in labor. They were sounds beyond shame.

175

Now she didn't struggle against him, didn't strike out against him.

Now, she drew him in.

She began to grapple him to her, to hook at him with her nails, gripping his shoulders as he moved above her. Then, as he thrust more gently, more slowly into her, she cried out "Oh—oh, dear *God!*" and swung her legs up to squeeze blindly at his thrusting hips for a moment, then to desperately wrap around him, hooking her ankles together neatly as any whore, to hold him to her as if she would never let him go.

It was getting to be time.

Link raised up and looked down between them, and saw that she was soaking—her cunt, the crack of her ass were slimy with fluids. Her privates seemed to have turned inside out—oily, puffed, slippery and shining deep red, seeming twice the size they had been before, so folded in, and neat, and furred closed.

She was crooning by then, a soft "Ohh . . .ooo . . ."

Link felt a gathering pleasure so great it was almost pain, a pleasure that locked him like a wrestling hold, and made his cock seem all the world. He moved on her faster, driving his cock in as if he were killing her with it, hearing her cries, and the rapid wet smacking sounds as their flesh met.

Then it was there, and he came.

He gritted his teeth to hold back a shout—and couldn't—and they cried out like children together, it felt so good as he pumped and pumped and pumped into her. He ached with it . . . it felt so fine.

Ad he still moved and moved on her, and the spunk was pumped in and oozed out of her, and ran down the wet rounds of her ass so they shone and glistened in the lamp-light.

176

"Dear Jesus . . ." he said, still in her, still moving a little in the wetness and warmth of her. "Jesus . . ." In that moment, as almost always for him, Link found himself loving the girl who had given him such great pleasure, who had made him such a splendid gift. He called her Nan, and kissed her throat.

CHAPTER 12

IN THE morning, she was gone.

Link drifted awake, cramped on the narrow cot, and saw the grey dawn light through the cell's open door. He rolled off the bunk, checked under it, and found the Bisley Colt's where he'd left it.

Lucky. Lucky she hadn't taken it into her head, from anger over his forcing her, or shame for the pleasure she'd found in it, to take his revolver and kill him with it.

A fair enough way to go, after all. And no more than he deserved for snoring through her waking and going. Getting old. There was a day she wouldn't have had time to slip off the cot, before he would have been full awake and had her in his hands.

Getting old.

And no doubt with a young man's trouble to look forward to today—or soon enough. Trouble arriving sufficient for a couple of young Buckskin Frank Leslies.

But for this morning, a long yawn and stretch . . . a rain-barrel bath out back, and a lumberjack's breakfast. Link had known men took care not to eat a thing when they thought they might be fighting. Worried a bullet might bust their breakfast out, inside; make trouble for the Dock. But Link figured a man already had more trouble than he could handle once his belly'd been busted, no matter what was inside it. He'd never seen his way to ducking a good breakfast; in fact, he thought it made him even more comfortable in a fight, having a good feed in him.

Ham and eggs first—then the Coes could take their turn.

He stretched again, rolled off the cot, and strolled, buck naked, out into the office. There was a small side door, double barred, and he opened it and walked out into the narrow alley. No decent woman should be back here to be shocked by a peep at his whang . . . whang was pretty wore out, anyway.

The mud was wet and cold between his toes, and Link considered that maybe the weather wasn't just right for rain-barreling, but he was feeling considerably sticky, and trudged on around the back, and there the son-of-a-gun was, green with moss and brim full of the coldest water in the territory.

There was no easy way.

Link took a grip with both hands on the barrel's rim, drew a deep breath, and with a grunt of effort heaved himself up and over the hoop-bound edge, and into the icy water with a splash.

"Ow—*Jesus!*" It knocked the breath out of him, it was so cold. But in was in—may as well get the benefit. He crouched down in the water, letting the chill blackness sweep over his head. Likely the way death was, something like this. He porpoised up with a gasp, and scrubbed with his hands at his legs and crotch, and his arm-pits. Then he ducked his head again and had had enough. Clean enough, by God, unless somebody volunteered a fine tin bath with flowers painted on it, a bar of Spanish soap, and a maid to bring up hot water.

He hauled himself up and out of the barrel in a cascade of freezing water, puffing and blowing like an old sport at a donkey-show. Teeth chattering, he high-stepped back down the narrow alley to the side door, and inside the office with a grunt of relief. The office pot-belly had ticked to ashes hours before, but there was some warmth there yet. Link got his clothes from the cell, and came back to the stove to dress.

It had been something of a night.

Double on the ham and four fried eggs. That would be the ticket.

The Rose was still asleep, smelling of empty, of cigar smoke and spilled beer. The old Chinaman wasn't up, but the colored swamper, George, was friendly enough once Link offered to help him bring in the stove wood. They sat down at the big kitchen table and had breakfast together like Christians; George had some ham, and a bowl of last night's stew—and Link, a ham steak big as a grizzly's paw, with four fried eggs sitting up on top of the meat in a row. That, and day-old biscuits to mop it up, and Link could push his chair back and feel himself satisfied.

Link sat a little longer in the warmth of the big kitchen stove, drinking coffee with no sugar and plenty of milk. He felt fine. Even that bout with the coaching girl hadn't hurt his side beyond a small ache or two. He'd been fucked out, slept in, and fed full up, and was the better for it. "Now, there's the way to brace up for a fight!" Holliday would have said, and would have been right, as usual. Nobody with him when he died in Denver. Some sorry sissy male nurse, was all . . .

Link missed, him. Nasty-looking little dentist. Only thing I care for in my profession, is the opportunity it

180

affords for the breathing of exhilarating gases . . . And, he'd once added, "the occasions those chemicals provide for messing with a lady there defenseless."

In the years he had known him, the few weeks he had spent gambling and whoring with him, Link had never known Holliday not do something that he wished to do and he certainly never did what he *didn't* care to do. As cheerfully self-willed as a child—a child who'd killed a dozen men or more, face to face with revolver or knife. Link had seen him kill that big cavalry sergeant. That had been something to see. Fellow had looked at the discards once too often. Big man, and dangerous, too, by report. He'd peeked once too often. "Well, I warned you!" that skinny little dentist had said, and risen out of his chair, hooked a finger in a cord around at the back of his collar, whipped out the cord and the straight razor fastened to the end of it, flipped open the razor as it came free, and reached with a sweep of his arm across the table to cut the sergeant across his stomach from hip-bone to hip-bone.

While all this was being done and done almost too fast to follow, the doomed man had had time to rise half up, and put his hands on the butt of his holstered revolver.

Then, his guts had been out on the table in a flood of blood.

"It has become a simple convenience to me, Bucky," Doc had said. "I find murder less exhausting than conversation." The man was a tragic education in himself, and wonderful company if he liked you.

Damned if he wouldn't be useful in this pickle. Three was heavy odds, and more than heavy if Reed and Billy Coe were good as they'd been cracked up to be, let alone that lunatic, Busey. Odd, the game that he and old Anse Coe were playing. They hadn't met and likely wouldn't meet, but they'd been playing a hard game, just the same, these last few days.

The old man had the edge; he had the men—his rannies, good enough in a bunch, and his sons, and the hired hand, Busey. A good edge, a good hand of poker for an old man to hold. Liked to run things; liked to make his money doing it. And more than willing for others to bleed in the getting done. Difficult to think of a man being fond of a son like that Charley—fat beast of a boy. Still, the old man must have some feelings. Not enough to weaken him in a fight, for sure.

Coe had the odds and Link had just one thing going. He knew who he was fighting. Coe didn't.

Link finished his coffee, scraped the chair back and stood up. "Old fellow," he thought, "win or lose, it will cost you more than you can pay." Link walked over to drop his coffee cup in the dish-tub, and went on out the back door into the yard. As he walked out to the necessary, he cut a fine and breezy fart.

He walked back toward the office down Main Street; it seemed to Link that Swazee's office was a good place to hole up until the Coes came in, if they weren't in town already. A marshal dead in a back alley was one thing. A marshal called out of his office to fight was something else. If the badge was to do him any good, make them brace him square, then he'd do better to act the lawman's part.

Swazee also kept a rack of long guns there. A Greener double-barrel ten-gauge might come in more than handy.

Link noticed, as he strolled along, that passers-by were giving him those quick sidelong glances, familiar now for many years. They were observing him, it might be, for future story-telling. Saw that drifter,

Link, ambling the town the morning the Coes killed him. Damn fool was cool as cabbage . . ."

Crossing James Street between two boardwalk stairs —and glad to see the mud was firming up from a couple of days of drying sunshine—Link was considerably startled by a young kid, a boy not more than eight years old, who came running down James Street lickey-split, saw Link, and swerved for him looking like he'd seen heaven. And this, as Link saw when the child came up to him, with a face full of tears.

"Marshal! *Marshal!*" And there he was, no taller than Link's watch chain, and needing the law. "My . . my mama . . . She sent me to get you. There's a man . . . messing with our stuff. And he won't quit!"

Link wondered how the hell Billy Tilghman kept his face straight throughout these kinds of doings. "Well, now," he said to the kid. "No reason to be weeping about it, is there?"

"He's sayin' . . . he's sayin' . . . bad things to my mama . . ." And up went the knuckles to meet the tears coming down.

"A foul-mouthed fellow, is he? Lord, boy, nothing for us to worry about in that." A small crowd had gathered, and was listening, but at a distance. Must have a reputation already. "Why don't you and me go see if we can make this fellow mind his manners— what say?"

He nodded to the boy and lead out, and the kid obediently turned and trotted away.

"That's Missus Turner's boy! They got a haberdasher!" A voice from the crowd.

As Link followed the boy down James Street, it occurred to him that this was just the kind of jape that the Coes, and particularly the madman, Busey, might enjoy arranging. On the chance of it, he'd have to stop carefully. Be nice to have that Greener already in his hand.

The kid trotted on up ahead, bringing the law to his mama's aid, and glancing back over his shoulder every now and again, much like a bird-dog ranging, to be sure that Link was keeping up. After fifty yards of hustling, Link saw the boy angle ahead toward a small sign that said: *Hats*. Must be the location of the abused mama . . .

CHAPTER 13

THE BOY had slowed enough—scared of being the first one in, more than likely—that Link was able to catch him by the shoulder before they could have come in view through the shop windows.

"Hold on, damn it! Is there a back way into your store?"

"Yes, sir—behind the smith's place." Boy seemed surprised to see the law so cautious.

"Don't want your mother hurt in a scramble, son," Link said, like an actor playing Hickok on the stage.

"Oh, yeah," said the kid.

"Show me that back way."

The boy led Link up onto the boardwalk, past racks of harness and a deal table piled with old pots and pans—the smith's mending, no doubt—and under a low doorway into a forge. The smith was there, a wide, small man, hairy as a bear and stripped to the waist. Two stooped albino helpers, likely his sons, were holding anvil work for him while he sized it up and hefted his hammer. The albinos were blinking and squinting their pink eyes in the glare of the forge fire. Seemed to Link they were in the wrong business.

The smith and his boys looked up as Link and the

185

boy came through, but they had nothing to say.

The boy led Link out of the back of the smithy, and through a gap in a high board fence. Link could see that the boy was enjoying the adventure more and more. No more tears.

Once through the fence, the boy turned to Link, put his finger to his lips, rounded his eyes, and pointed to a plank door, once painted blue. The fatal haberdashery.

Link likely disappointed the boy detective once again by now drawing his revolver and rushing in to the rescue. Instead, he took a long look around the cluttered little yard and at the few dirty windows that looked down into it. There might be extra trouble waiting there, but he saw no sign at all of it.

The boys were staring up at him with a disillusioned pout. Caution and cowardice all smelled the same to him, it seemed.

"That man . . . the one bothering your mama, was he alone?"

An impatient nod. Boy wanted to see some action, that was clear.

Link sighed, opened the blue door, and stepped in.

Two things struck him at once: a smell of boiling sizing-glue, and a rich, rolling Irish brogue. He was standing in a crowded little closet of a room, jammed with sheets of wool felt and fur felt, leather strips and ribbon spools, and an untidy heap of wooden head forms, clamps and stretchers.

It was a hattery, not a haberdashers.

The sizing stink came from a pint pot of glue boiling away on a tiny sheet-iron stove against the wall. And through a stained calico curtain came the brogue.

The boy, who'd come in behind him and who now seemed less dauntless, stood by the back door and pointed at the curtains. That, it seemed, was the voice that said bad things to mamas. And so it was.

"Sez me to meself, if there's a rip needs stuffin' by a foine bucko dancer, sure it is yer own, Miz Turner. Oi know what a widow duz with her little hands at night . . . (apparently demonstrating) an' oi got the root ta stop that there itch fer yuz!"

Link stepped quietly to the curtain, parted it a hair, and looked through the slit.

A gandy dancer, sure enough. Link had seen enough of that sort of Irishmen when he hunted meat for the railroad. A big fellow, white-skinned and freckle-faced, with the muscle-hunched shoulders and spade-wide hands that grew from that labor. This one was black haired, odd with his freckles, and blue eyed. Would have been a good looking fellow, but for missing his upper teeth in front. He had the long lip and bully's air of his kind, and no doubt was tough enough when it came to fist fighting.

"Look at it, now, darlin', take a look-see at this."

Had his jock out, and was waving it at the poor woman. She was a small, thin woman, with handsome eyes, shocked and frightened now. She was backed up against a case of hats as far as she could go, and the Hibernian Hero was facing her, his pants open, making fucking movements with his hips.

"Like a taste of it, would ya?" He was stepping on some fallen hats; must have been trying them on, drunk, when a better idea had occured to him.

Link tugged the star off his shirt, tossed it to the staring little boy, picked the glue pot off the stove, and stepped through the curtain into the store. "Got yore sizin' Miz Turner," he sang out stupid as any rube, and walked down the aisle and to them, grinning and amiable, apparently unconscious of any such thing as a big drunken Irishman with his cock in his hand.

The Irishman turned on him with considerable speed, let go his privates, and doubled his fists. "Yuz friggin' scut," he said, his face flushed red and took a quick long step to Link, struck at him with a left lead, and swung a right to break his jaw.

Link swayed away from the left which was thrown hard and fast (the fellow was good with his fists) and when the right came in, ducked under it and tossed the pint of boiling glue onto the Irishman's cock.

The result was wonderful—better than a play. The big laborer froze, his long right arm still extended. He stood stock still for nearly a second, then looked down.

Link had seen some capering in his day, Papagoes and Commanche, and some drunk sailors off a British man o' war. But he'd never seen a jig the equal of this.

The fellow bayed like a dog in bright moonlight, and commenced to caper about the little store like a madman. The dripping glue steamed and smoked on his flying whang, and he would pause sometimes in midair to try and touch it, soothe it, make it well.

It was unseemly, but Link couldn't help it. He began to laugh and couldn't stop. The big Irishman screamed and battered about the shop, begged for a priest, leaped for the door, fumbled for the latch and couldn't wait to grasp it—put his head down and butted his way through in a splinter of glass and wood, then staggered out onto the walkway, howling and trying to hold himself with scorched fingers until he stumbled over the boardwalk edge and fell to the street below, apparently heading for a distant horse trough for relief.

A crowd, which had followed Link and the boy at a discreet distance, observed all this with considerable satisfaction, and Link, assuring the woman that all was well and over, found her unwilling or unable to answer him. She stood amidst her trodden hats with her face buried in her hands, and wouldn't pay any mind, not even to her boy. A lady, apparently, though poor.

No one followed Link back to his office—must have felt they'd already had their money's worth for the morning. He'd had a wrestle, getting his badge back from the boy. Kid apparently thought it was a gift.

Well, if this was the law business, no wonder so many sissies and bullies went in for it—a dozen of them for every man like Smith or Tilghman. There was not that much to it, really; if a fellow made a fool of himself, you beat him. Link imagined that the courtroom made it all more complicated, but surely not much. It was a question, then, of who was paying the judge the most—the politicians, or the accused.

A bad business, all in all. Old Swazee was welcome to his badge, if he ever climbed out of his bed to claim it, which he likely would, if Charmian had anything to say about it.

The office was dark, and empty. He'd half expected Nancy Plum to be there with a kiss, or a coach whip. But it was empty.

He tried the door key to Swazee's gun cabinet, and found that it was unlocked. Not much in the way of thieving in Colt Creek, apparently. Link had known towns where Wesley Hardin would have been robbed of his guns and watch if he'd tilted his head back to down a shot of whiskey.

There was a Remington rifle in the cabinet, and a Winchester rifle—one of the new ones—a more powerful cartridge than the Henry sported. And there were two shotguns. No Greeners, but one better than fair L.C. Smith, a twelve-gauge double. It was a much used piece, with a battered stock and the bluing rubbed off the side of the barrels.

Link rummaged in the cabinet drawers and found three folded up *Police Gazettes* (hidden by old Swazee, no doubt, from Charmian's eyes) two pairs of clean socks, a bunch of loose Ohio Blue Tip matches, and several handfuls of cartridges and shells, among which were five single-ought buck shells in twelve-gauge.

That would do nicely.

Link sat down in the busted-back armchair behind Swazee's desk, set the shotgun on the desk top, checked it—it was clean enough—and slipped in two shells. He closed the action carefully—it was a hammerless model—and leaned back with the shotgun in his lap.

Time to do nothing but wait.

There was a limit to the days the Coes could let go by before they called him to account if they wanted to keep the running of the town. The brothers were back, and they'd brought another killer with them. Have to do something with those guns, and likely today, or men in Colt Creek might start getting big ideas about running their own town.

And, of course, they didn't know but what Link had his own ambitions that way. Might be pleasant, owning a town. Certain to be profitable, and not bad doings for a man who walked into Colt Creek with a lame brown horse and some loose change in his pocket . . .

If he could get away with it. If he wanted to get away with it.

Just something to think about, waiting . . . Link settled deeper into Swazee's chair. Give the old man credit, his butt had shaped a mighty comfortable sitting-pit in this chair.

It slowly stretched into a long day.

Not unpleasant. Link had found that, lately, he

could enjoy just sitting, remembering old times. People. Getting older was what it was, of course. Didn't kid himself about that. There was a day he went from morning to night—from morning *through* the night, as often as not—about as fast and as tough as a locomotive could.

Not any longer. Had neither the fire for it, nor the dumb to do it. Cared for nothing, then, except maybe showing people what a devil of a fellow Frank Leslie was. And did show a few, at that. It didn't hurt to have a skill with pistols that far passed the average and a strong wrist for a knife as well. And—used to be—a good eye for a poker deal. No small advantages. And he'd stretched them about as far as they could be stretched.

Robbed a bank in Nagoles, once. There was a lark! The old Mex guard had peed in his pants when Allison, already a wild Texan then, but not yet a drunken murderer, had fired a shot into the ceiling. The bank people had given over the money without a fuss—the paper money. They wouldn't give up the gold. It was the damndest thing, here were four fast guns . . . him and Omahundro and Allison. Three fast guns then, not counting Jack Rye, who couldn't shoot worth a damn. There they were, three fierce young badmen though new to robbing, and the old Mexican who ran the bank had gone behind his teller cages himself to pick up the paper pesos, stack it all, and pass it over the counter to them.

"What's this shit?" said Omahundro, "you dirty Greaser!" And he put the muzzle of his revolver right up against the old man's head and threw a wink to the generality. "Where's that God-damned gold?"

The old banker had drawn himself up like a king. "The gold, *señor*," he'd said in better English than

Jack's was, "the gold is of our nation's earth, and you may not have it."

Allison had just laughed, but Omahundro was goggle-eyed. He'd just shot two men to death in a fight in Fort Worth, and was feeling fresh and fierce.

"I am goin' to blow your blankety-blank brains out right here on this blankety-blank dirt floor, you old fart, if you don't trot those yellow-boys right out!" And he meant it.

Allison was laughing, and didn't care, but Frank had felt some admiration for the old man. The Mexicans were hard into one of their revolutions, and he'd caught the spirit of the thing.

So, "Say Jack," he said—to Omahundro, not Jack Ray—"is it true you have Mex blood in you?"

That got Omahundro turned around in a hurry, and mad. "What are you saying—that I've got damn Greaser blood in me?"

Frank had shaken his head. "Hell no, I don't think that, but I heard Billy Buttons swore to it on his death-bed." Billy'd been a celebrated sissy and man-midwife in south Texas.

"Now, God-damnit," said Omahundro, grinding his teeth. "It's a lie!"

"Way I heard it, it was a Mex banker was the Dad." By this time, Allison was laughing fit to bust. "So," Frank had said, "You better look out you don't shoot your own Daddy."

As often happened, all the talk and japing had cooled things down to where there was no shooting. They'd all been . . . what? Nineteen years old? Not even that much. He'd been seventeen; Omahundro eighteen, if that. And they'd not been as mean as they fancied themselves, either. Dangerous enough, but not really mean. That had come later, and for Allison, more than the rest.

Strange how different the Texans were. A different people, really. And he'd made bad enemies among them. Enough, and bad enough, so that some of them would come after him, if they knew where he was. Would come after him knowing his true name, and not be afraid of it. Those people were slow forgetters . . .

Link shifted in the chair. Swazee had done a good job of breaking it in, but there was a wild spring in there still. Well, that had been the big bank robbery. Had netted them three-hundred Mexican Government paper pesos, enough, just barely, for two days for the four of them (Sam Paley had held the horses) at the Hibiscus, a whorehouse in Renosa so low that not even soldiers—not even policemen would go to it.

Well, he'd robbed this and that since, the last being MacDuff's cash drawer, but no more banks. He didn't like taking what didn't belong to him. He could do it, but he didn't like it. Made him feel ashamed. No career for an armed robber with that kind of weak belly.

So he'd become a gambler, and a pimp, a sport, Fancy-man, and killer. Just the sort of career to suit a wild boy with scruples. And he had little complaint about it—had had the best of that sort of life, probably and in the best of times for it . . .

By afternoon, he was tired of waiting.

It was the wise thing to do, no doubt, but mighty tedious. If they were going to come straight for him, they'd have already done it. Sad fact was, old Anse had probably told them to tease him out a little, see if they could catch him with his new badge down. And if that was so, they'd take their time about him, just take their time.

Well, it was a poor game, but it was one that two could play. If chance was the fashion, he'd wear it.

CHAPTER 14

HE WENT to the gun cabinet, unloaded the Smith, and put the shotgun away. No use looking the coward by parading around the town all day with it. Damn thing was liable to go off if he set it down too hard, anyway. Didn't care much for a hammerless gun—couldn't tell what the damn things were doing.

As he closed the glass-paned cabinet door, Link caught sight of his reflection. Always surprised at how old he was looking; didn't feel that damn old . . . The scar down that cheek certainly did mar his looks. Talk all you like about the romance of a dashing scar, piratical looks and all that; the reality was likely to be plain ugly. What he might be able to use was another revolver. That might come in handy.

Outside, the day was clouding up—mackerel clouds, they used to call them, high-up flat ripples of clouds. It didn't look like rain, thank God; the streets had just dried out.

By his reflection, it seemed he could use a haircut—get himself barbered up for whatever transpired. Link turned left, down Main. He'd passed a striped pole around the corner, a block or two down. Get a shave and a haircut, any sporting news available. He'd heard that Dixon, the Negro lightweight, had died, or been hurt. Be interesting to see if that was so. Fine fighter, that boy. Link held no stock in the nonsense about the niggers' heads being thicker than whites. He'd cracked enough heads, white and otherwise, to know they were all about as tender.

It was said that Dixon had the fastest left seen since the English fighter, Cribb. But Cribb had fought so long ago, who could tell? And Cribb had been twice Dixon's size; must have been slower. That Irishman this morning had been handy. Stood too straight when he swung, though—you could tell the man was no professional. Well, what about Corbett? Stood straight as a string . . . Exception that proved the rule, like Hardin's draw out of shoulder holsters. Shoulder holsters!

Link was almost to the corner turn-off, when a man came bustling up to him, in a flurry and out of breath.

"Say, Marshal!"

If it was that Irishman, or another like him, the hell with them!

"Marshal, I'm in the way of business down the street, and Henry Forster won't move his goods!"

"Now, what in the world do you expect me do to, Mister?"

"Why, make him move those hides! They're keepin' any customers at all from gettin' into my place!"

"I don't . . ."

"He don't own the whole damn street, do he? All I want is for you go tell him."

Link shifted as if to walk around the fellow, who was full-bearded, and sweaty as a running horse. But the man shifted right along with him, to keep him from getting away.

"All I want is for you to come tell him."

"Where is this damn shop of yours?"

"Now it's right down the street. Right there!"

And there it was, down further and across from the barber shop, as a matter of fact. Link could see a harness shop and a stack of hides on the boardwalk steps just in front of it.

"*What's* your damn shop, I said?"

"Why," the bearded man said, "I have the Bon Ton! The ice cream parlor!" He seemed put out that Link had had to ask. Well, it did put another face on things. A soda parlor. Damned if he wouldn't have a dish after his haircut. By God, that was waiting out a fight in style!

"All right," he said to the bearded fellow, "I'll see he gets those hides out of there if you'll stand me a dish of your best."

A sweaty handshake. "You just made yourself a deal, Marshal." He led Link down the street in triumph. A small crowd followed them at a distance, probably hoping for a repeat of the morning's entertainment.

If so, they were mighty disappointed. Link walked up to the pile of hides, and called to a rabbity fellow with a pencil behind his ear and an apron on, who was counting over some good in front of the leather shop.

"Say, there!"

"Yes, sir?" says the rabbit.

"You get your employer out here."

The rabbit ducked into the store, and, after a minute, came out following a very small, upright man in a good grey suit.

"What's all this about, Officer?" he said, eyeing Link's badge with a skeptical air. Link had seen this fellow's type many times. An upstanding citizen, with no opinion at all of gunmen, with or without badges. He looked to be in a hurry to get back to his business.

"Those hides are blocking the stairs there," Link

said. "Be a good idea if you moved them."

"Good lord," the small man—Mr. Forster, apparently—said. "Why the devil didn't you ask me to move them, George?"

"I did! And you . . ."

"Just move those hides, Mister Forster, if you will," Link said.

Forster nodded in a weary way, said, "Move them, Roger," to the rabbit, and went back inside.

"Now, that's more like it," said the ice cream parlor owner. "Marshal, come on in and get your dish of fine."

"In a while," Link said, tipped his hat, and went off across the street through a disappointed crowd to get his haircut.

The majesty of the law.

Billing's Tonsorial was a tony little ken, aping its betters in bigger towns. Mister Billings had taken pains with it. White tile on the floor for the sweepings, mirrors down one wall of the narrow place, pictures of prize fighters and actresses glued neatly onto the opposite wall, and to top all, three genuine crank-up and spin-around barber chairs. There was a big rubber plant in the corner, and a round-top table under the picture of Lillian Russell in the almost altogether, was piled with old copies of *Sporting News*, and *Police Gazette*.

A comfortable place. And empty except for one customer in the first chair, an old man just getting a few last flourishing snips to the top of his head, where seven long white hairs marched across his bare scalp side by side. There was only one barber in the place, an odd-looking fellow with Macassar-soaked black hair, and a little waxed mustache.

"Be right with you," says this chap, glancing at

Link's badge, and Link settled into the second chair to wait his turn. After a bit, he thought of getting up for one of the *Sporting News*, but it seemed too much trouble.

The barber, apparently Mr. Billings, kept up a light running chatter with the old man while he made clicking passes with his scissors over the old fellow's head, cutting not a hair that Link could see. They were talking about a local stake-race run before Link had gotten to town; since it was a particular conversation, he stayed out of it, relaxed in the chair, which was a dandy, looked for Lily Langtry's picture on the opposite wall (he'd known her from San Francisco, once—in the Biblical Sense, as Holliday would have said), and enjoyed the odors of hair oil, hot towels, and Bay Rum.

Civilization was what those smells said.

Finally the gaffer was done, hauled himself up out of his chair, put on his coat and hat, paid three bits flat, and tottered on out the fancy glass-paneled door.

Billings sighed, probably at the no tip despite all the friendly conversation, and signed for Link to stay in the second chair when he made a movement to get up.

"A haircut and a shave," Billings said, after giving Link's head a good look. "And desperate in need of both, Marshal."

"I admit it," Link said.

The barber cranked the chair back to an easy recline, took a folded sheet ouf of a cupboard and shook it out. Link noticed it was fresh laundered, the first clean barber's sheet he'd seen since Boise—and draped it over, tucking an end of it neatly into Link's collar. All the particularity was pretty encouraging, though Link had known finicky barbers who had a very rough hand with the razor.

Billings put out a soft finger, and rubbed Link's

beard stubble the wrong way, with a couple of quick cat's-paw strokes. "Hot towel," he said, not asking.

"O.K.," Link said, though he hadn't been asked.

Link leaned back at ease, relaxed under the striped sheet, and closed his eyes. He considered the possibility that the Coes might have declined on a waiting game, after all. Bide their time and then, do him. Wait a week, two weeks—a month, if they cared to.

It didn't make sense. The longer it went, the worse for them. That was a fact, and Anse Coe seemed the old man to face facts. He wondered if the thought of that delay had appealed to him . . . if he were getting a little shy as he got older. Of course, he didn't hunt for trouble as he had years ago. Didn't seem to have to— trouble found him out fast enough.

Billings plucked a towel out of the round, tin heater in a wisp of steam, flapped it a couple of times to cool it just a bit, and turned to drape it neatly around Link's face, leaving just the right eye-nose-and-mouth space in the center. The towel was almost too hot, but not quite.

A class ken, indeed. A parlor of this quality made a better town of Colt Creek. He took a deep breath, letting his muscles loosen, feeling small clinks along his back as the small bones of his spine shifted.

Better than riding trail by a long shot.

A bang and rattle at the door made him open his eyes.

Company.

A very tall man, gawked and gangling as a scarecrow, and dressed like an undertaker in a black clawhammer coat and tall stove-pipe hat, slammed the door behind him, rattling the glass in it, and said, "Well met, Luther!" to the barber, as he took off his coat and then his high hat, and hung them neatly on the clothes tree beside the door. He wore two Colt's Peacemaker .44's in crossed gunbelts, grips forward for cross-draws.

Considerable artillery, for an undertaker.

Link drew his revolver, under the sheet, while the tall man's back was still turned, and laid the Colt's along his thigh. Just habit.

"Day, Mister Coe," the barber said in an odd voice, and Link turned his head with the towel still wrapped around his face, and saw that the barber had gone white as cheese whey, so that his black hair and small mustache looked false as a clown's. He glanced Link's way and Link had time to give him one murderous look before the tall man, undoing his string tie, turned from the clothes tree to the empty first chair.

He nodded to Link as he sat down, folding into the chair like a great carpenter's rule, and settling himself into the ease of it, as Link had done. He wore fine clothes, a white linen shirt and black wool trousers. His boots were Mexican, high-topped and tooled.

"No shave, Luther," he said, "Haircut'll do me." He had a deep, humming voice, like an actor's.

The barber didn't answer for a moment, and Link's hand tightened on the Bisley Colt's. Then Billings muttered, "O.K.," and began to fuss with his scissors and such behind them.

Link felt his heart thudding in his chest like a donkey engine pumping at a mine. What had MacDuff said? Reed Coe—something about Reed Coe being a long drink of water—a bony fellow . . .

Luck.

His luck had come back to him.

"My God, Luther," the tall man said to the barber, "I hear there's been a storm of the most dreadful violence in our town while I've been gone!"

The barber mumbled something, and Link heard

201

the nervous stutter of his scissors. Link didn't turn his towel-wrapped head to look at him; he was watching Reed Coe out of the corner of his eye.

Coe had a long, knobby face like a horse's, as mobile as an actor's. It matched his voice. "I understand we now have barkeep law in the Creek," he said to the barber, and made a humerous face to Link. "and," he continued with a comically mournful expression, "I understand—though I can scarcely believe it—that my beloved half-brother, our plump and temperamental young Charley, has been brutally done to death!" He tilted his head back, squinting up at Billings. "A tragedy, isn't it?"

Billings cleared his throat, tried to say something, and nodded.

"That boy," the gangling man said, "that sweet, sweet boy! The old man is heartbroken about it. *Heartbroken*. Don't think he'll be able to bear it, Luther. I fear Charley's passing is going to be the death of our old Daddy." He chuckled as Billings unfolded a striped sheet and draped it over him, and cut a smiling glance at Link. "Say, Luth," he said, "you better tend to our friend, here; man's waiting for his shave."

"I'm in no hurry," Link said, and saw the light glitter off the scissors in the barber's trembling hand. "Towel's plenty hot."

"Now, that's white of you, Mister," Reed Coe said, "mighty white. As for me—well, truth to tell, I'm presently getting duded up for an affair of honor. A brother and a friend and I are forced to execute justice upon the person of a bartender." He cocked an eye up at Billings. "Well, Luth? Get to it! But leave the Burnsides; a lady whose opinion I cherish has told me they're becoming." He rolled an eye at Link. "And we are, of course, at the ladies' order in these matters."

202

Billing's scissors and comb began to click.

"Now, what surprised me, I may tell you," Coe went on, after a pause while the barber worked, "is not the demise of Fat Charley. What astonished me, Luther, is that any stray drifter scraping beers should come along and do in Ike Stern! Did that surprise you, too, Luther?"

Billings cleared his throat, and said, "Yes."

"Well, it surprised me. Ike was never very fast, but he was certainly *steady*, wouldn't you say so?" He chuckled and shook his head, while the barber lifted his scissors up out of the way. "And here I am, untimely ripped from the fleshpots of Boise, forced, with Billy—and our friend—to locate this very odd sort of deputy, and kill him." He sighed. "It's bound to be noisy." He turned to Link. "Did you know, Mister—Mister—?"

"Just call me 'Fred,'" Link said. "Just passin' through."

"Well, did you know, Fred—you know that the Turks take a blessedly silent bowstring to persons who've become troublesome?" He slid his hands out from under the barber's sheet, and demonstrated. "They wrap the bowstring so . . . and then a steady hard pull . . . All quiet as a snowfall. And here we are, citizens of the finest land God Almighty has placed upon the earth, still using firearms to make all this damn noise."

"Why, that's true," Link said.

"Luth, damn it, will you stop pecking at my head, and give Fred here his shave?"

"No hurry," Link said. "I'm in no hurry at all."

"Hmmm . . . all right, keep snipping, Luther." He turned to Link. "Of course," he said, "these noisy turns are coming to an end. It'll all be lawyers, soon. The damn lawyers will work quiet as any bowstring.

203

Right, Luther? Like my oily cousin, Wilse."

"Right," the barber said.

"Wilse," Reed Coe said to Link, "is a Yale man—which is much the same as calling him a sneak-thief directly." He threw back his head to laugh, and the barber again lifted his scissors out of the way. "Say now, Luth," Coe said, settling back in the chair with his hands folded comfortably on his stripe-sheeted chest, "we just stopped by this fellow's office and he'd scampered! He'll toss that badge away for sure, and go to earth like a run fox. Damned if I know what the fellow looks like! Cap' duFrene told Billy. But you know Billy—from what he says, the damn lurcher could be either Edwin Booth or Quasimodo!"

"I've seen him," Link said. "I've seen him more than once." He put his left foot down on the floor, and slowly swiveled his chair to face the side of Coe's.

"Have you, by God! And what does this bad man look like?"

"Oh . . . about my size," Link said, shifting the Bisley slightly under the sheet.

"Yes?"

"Well set-up man, not nearly tall as you."

"Few are," Coe said.

"Grey eyes—dark grey, I believe. Grey in his hair, too. Fellow's no spring chicken."

"Not likely to get older, though," Coe said. "It'll be a favor to him."

"Wears a Bisley Colt's on his right hip, barrel slanted in a bit."

"Does he, now? Quite the fancy Dan!" He smiled. "You're being very helpful. Has this type ruffled your feathers?"

"No, the fellow hasn't bullied me. Seems stuck on himself, that's all."

Coe made a rueful face. "Well, that's a sin we all practice. It was, after all, by pride the angels fell." He sighed, then gave Link a cold glance. "Anything else to tell me about him?"

"Yes," Link said. "He has a long scar . . ." He reached up with his left hand, tugged the damp towel from his face, and dropped it on the floor. ". . . down his cheek."

Coe sat still, staring at him.

"It does appear," he said after a moment, with a wry smile, "that I have been making an extraordinary jackass of myself." His long face was flushed red.

"We've all done that," Link said.

"But not, I believe, in quite such . . . delicate circumstances." He glanced down at his hands, folded on the sheet. "My present posture appears all too appropriate. You would not, I suppose, care to adjourn to the street for a more—sporting—start?"

"No," Link said.

"Thought not," Coe said. "I certainly wouldn't, in your place." And he moved.

He gripped the sheet that covered him, flung it billowing up into the air, and behind that fragile, momentary barrier, slid fast as a snake out of the barber's chair and made a wickedly fast cross-draw of his left gun just before Link, aiming through the fluttering sheet at Coe's silhouette, shot him through the body.

Coe grunted and got off his shot as the sheet fell away. It struck Link's chair-back just beside his head, and blew a piece of it away. The sounds of the shots slammed and hammered from the walls, and Link went out of his chair and onto one knee and shot Coe again, a little higher, into his ribs. It knocked the tall man turning so that his reply blasted wide and broke a basin with a crack. The room was dark with smoke and the smell of it. Link shot Coe again, giving him no chance to recover, to set himself. The bullet hit the gangling man in his chest, broke a bone inside him with a snap, and pushed him back into the barber's door. Coe's gun dropped from his right hand, and as he fell into the glass panels and broke them, he made another swift cross-draw, pulled his right gun, and fired it. The slug banged into the floor just in front of Link and stung his feet through his boot soles.

The door smashed as Coe fell into it, and the tall man struggled and stomped in a tangle of broken frame and glass splinters. He shouted something, and blood flew out of his mouth and spattered his white shirt, but gunfire had deafened Link so that he couldn't hear what Coe shouted. The tall man raised his revolver, but his arm was driven through by glass and he couldn't tug it free to aim. Link shot him through the chest again, firing into the smoke—and felt the sting as his barber's sheet ignited from the muzzle blasts he'd fired through it. He tore the sheet away, and saw Reed Coe dying in the door. The tall man, gazing dreaming down, slowly folded and fell in a welter of shattering glass. A splinter caught his face and pulled his cheek out on a point and sliced clear through it as he slid into a huddle on the jamb.

The narrow room seemed to echo gunshots.

The gunsmoke stung Link's eyes, as he stood and walked over to where Reed Coe lay.

"My door," the barber said, then turned and vomited against the wall.

Coe's corpse settled as Link stood over it. A liquid sound came from it, and then a smell of shit. Link thought that there wasn't much that Gold almighty himself could do that was more important than the killing of a man like this. It was a large thing to have done, with nothing but a forty-dollar revolver. He bent down, took Coe's Peacemaker from his hand, reloaded the spent round and tucked the weapon into his own waistband. Then he reloaded the Bisley, and holstered it.

He stepped over Reed Coe, and walked out onto the boardwalk, leaving bloody bootprints. There was no one there, and the street was empty, as well. Across the way, he saw the hide merchant, Forster, locking up his shop.

Colt Creek was bracing for a blow.

He went down the boardwalk steps, crossed the street, and climbed the steps to the Bon Ton Ice Cream Parlor. He rattled the door until the bearded man came out of the back of his shop to open it.

"I'll have a dish of vanilla," Link said.

CHAPTER 15

WHEN HE finished his ice cream, Link left the parlor, and started walking up toward Main. The vanilla cream had been very good—good as he'd ever tasted. It was peculiar, what a great distance separated the living and the dead. The greatest distance of all, and the least. It would have been enjoyable if he and Reed Coe had been playacting their parts as Coe seemed so suited to do, and could, once all the noise was over, walk out of Billing's Tonsorial together, and take a dish of ice cream at the Bon Ton.

Enjoyable.

Link wondered what Coe had shouted there, as he was dying, shot to pieces in the doorway. A curse? Perhaps. Or a joke, since he was a humorous fellow. And a fine hand with the pistols, too. Faster than Stern. He'd that knack—the only way, really, to cross-draw quickly. A nice, smooth, circular motion to the revolver and out with it. It was no good grabbing straight for the piece. You had, in a way, to go the long way around, to get the best speed. Coe's first draw had been hidden by his flung sheet—a nice try, only thing he could have tried—but Link had seen the second draw clearly. That swift, sure, curved track to it. Man had done a lot of practicing. It was the weakness of the cross-draw, that you had to get it perfect, and then practice. Every day.

Probably a good shot, too, though Link had given him no chance to prove it. Ambushed the poor fellow, really. Caught him out and killed him.

At Main, Link crossed the street, climbed up to the boardwalk, and walked toward the Rose. It was late, now. Late enough in the afternoon so that the sun had sunk behind the buildings' false fronts. Be getting dark in half an hour or so.

There were few people on the street, and those few all men—no women or kids at all. A few men hurrying about their business after a quick look at him. Some dogs lounging along. The dogs didn't bother to peep at the Great Man-killer.

Link smelled the gunsmoke still clinging to his clothes.

No need to start feeling badly about it just because the fellow had something to him. What he had done to Coe, Coe would gladly have done to him, barber's towel and all and made a joke of it, besides. Coe must have made a fool of many men before he killed them— it was the nature of the man.

No need to feel badly about the fellow.

And better not feel that you hold all aces now, either. One dead, but two to kill, and neither one an easy mark. Link was more concerned about the madman than Reed Coe's brother. Billy Coe was not likely to be faster, smarter, or tougher than Reed had been. And even if he were, not likely to be fast, smart or tough enough. The madman, Busey, was a different matter.

Link had had to do with one or two deranged men. He'd found it best to be very direct with them—to deal with them straight or leave them alone. Once had run like a cur dog from a man in a mining camp who'd thought he was a devil and had already proved it twice, by murdering people with a pitch-fork, stabbing them to death through their tent walls as they slept. It had made for an uneasy night, tent-sleeping, listening for soft footsteps on the other side of moonlit canvas. Fellow—and no-one had the least notion who it was—had left his mark on Link's tent canvas one night. Two horns of the devil, painted in red.

Link had pulled stakes next morning.

Something of the same thing here, except there'd be no running form this pitch. He would have liked to have taken the madman first in the fight, dealt with the second man second. But it wouldn't wash. Billy Coe'd be too good to let stand while he killed Busey. If he could get them one at a time, wait a bit . . .

Might be Reed's death would shake them. Charley gone, now Reed. Might shake them . . .

Reed had joked in his barber chair about their dad missing Charley. Well, Charley's loss might have been something of a joke to the Coes—be doubtful if the old man would feel so jolly about losing Reed. Old Anse Coe had only one of his fierce sons left. Not much to joke about, there.

Holding a territory with three killers, all blood kin, was one thing. Holding it with two of those shot to death, was another.

Link doubted the old man was up to it. Using Busey was a sign how near the bottom of the barrel was.

Link paused at the corner of Main and Clark. The Rose was only a block away and there was a good chance they'd both be there. They'd have heard about Reed by now. Likely they'd decide to do nothing at all.

Stay together, let him come to them. Let him make the first move.

It was what he'd do, were he in their boots. Stay tucked in the Rose, don't wander, and wait for the barkeep Deputy to come swaggering in.

Link turned on his heel, and walked away down Main. If waiting was in fashion, and he thought it would be, then by God he'd wait them out till hell froze over. Wait till that madman would wait no longer. Then they'd come for him, whether Billy Coe cared to nor not. Busey was unlikely to be a patient man.

He turned at the corner of Monroe street, and walked down toward Swazee's office. It was too bad the old man had been so sorely hurt; he was certainly no gunfighter, but he might have been handy, none the less. Come to think of it, Charmian Swazee would probably be of more use. Tougher.

Nobody out on this street at all. No loafers, nobody. Appeared that curiosity had limits, after all. Which went to show how well the Coes had tamed Colt Creek. Link had seen towns where children came to gunfights to get blood on their handkerchiefs to show off at school. Colt Creek, up to now, at any rate, had been peaceful as Philadelphia, providing you went along with the Coes.

Link paused at the office door and tested it. Locked. He took out his key, unlocked the door, then stepped in quickly, his hand on the butt of the Bisley.

The office was empty—dark, as usual, in the fading light. The memories of last night came back to him—the smoothness of her, her smells. Sounds she had made . . . By God, he wouldn't be caught short if these two did kill him. Couldn't complain he'd missed a pleasure, that was certain. Forced her, of course, no matter if she did end by liking it.

"Means and ends," Holliday used to say. "I can only tell the difference by the smell. One's *slightly* fishier!"

There was a man who'd have come in handy about now. Holliday would have liked Reed Coe. Same kind of fellow. But Holliday would never have missed the *feelings* of a man about to try and kill him, hot towel on the fellow's face, or not.

He went to the small table, dug his match-safe from his vest pocket, and lit the kerosene lantern. And he had just realized that it didn't belong there, that he had carried it into the cell last night, when the voice came from behind his back.

"You're very careless, for a man in your line of business."

Link turned around slowly, keeping his hand clear of his revolver. "Careless," was right. Careless enough to have killed him. He'd forgotten the small side door.

Nancy Plum stood in the deep shadow of the cell door. She wore trousers and shirt and her coaching vest; her hair was drawn up under an old dent-crowned Stetson. She carried a Spencer carbine cradled in her arms.

"Figuring on using that piece on me, were you?"

"I sure thought about doing just that," she said, and started to say something more, but didn't. She came to the table, and put the short rifle down. Then, she said, "I could have killed you from in there; if I'd been Billy Coe, you'd have been dead as a doornail."

"Yes," Link said, pulling out one of the cane bottom chairs for her to sit in, "I surely would have been." Then he sat down too, and watched her, wondering what had brought her to him. Not some sudden affection, he hoped. It was not the time for it, nor was he the man. He'd seen many a virgin, just broken in, come kissing at the fellow that had done them. Had happened to him many a time, and never satisfactorily. For girls like that, just passed past their first time fucked, there seemed to be a machinery inside them that required it become a loving attachment.

The wrong time. And the wrong man.

"I owe you a deep apology, Miss Plum . . ."

"Nancy," she said. "You could call me Drivin' Nan . . ."

"Well, I'm very sorry about what I did last night. I was rough with you . . ."

"I don't care," she said, leaning across the table, staring at him with bright grey eyes. "I did care last night, but now I don't. I'm here . . ." She thumped on the table-top with her small fist. "I'm here to back your play against the Coes."

For a moment, Link could only sit and stare at her.

"How the hell old are you, anyway?" The damn young fool had come to play Wild West!

"Old enough to know what I'm doing," she said. "You need some help. You need another gun! And I'm a good shot with a rifle!"

Link had to restrain himself. Keep from leaning across the table and hitting her, for making a fool game of it all.

"Now,' he said, "you listen to me . . ."

"The Coes have run out their string," she said to him. "They've come boring down on people long enough, and it's time to clean 'em up!"

Damn that Ned Buntline!

Link reached across the table, got hold of her wrist, and gripped it hard enough to shut her up. "Now, you listen to me. This is no damn game! An old man got

213

burned on a hot stove, two men got their insides shot out and now another one's dead as well."

"Who?" she said, mouth open, a child listening to a story. "Who?"

"Reed Coe."

She made an "O" with her mouth. "Jumpin' Jesus!" she said. "You shot Reed Coe?" She sat, thinking, ignoring his hand on her arms. Then she looked up at him, studying him in the lantern light. "Why, this is a famous fight," she said. "Everybody's going to hear about it, back East and everything! You got to let me help. I can help you!"

There was no use talking to her, telling her that Billy Coe, or Busey, or any man like them would slaughter her as quickly and as casually as a man struck a horse-fly from his mount's neck. Rifle, revolver, made no difference. All she might accomplish would be his own death as he tried to protect her.

She was a child, full of foolish romance, and there was no use talking to her.

He got up, still holding her wrist, and pulled her toward the open cell door. It was a moment before she realized what he intended to do. Then she fought him —kick, scream, and bite, fought him hard as she had the night before, until he wrestled her into the cell, slammed the door, almost catching her hand as she tried to struggle out, and barred it.

Then she raved and cursed and called him a filthy disgusting thing that had forced himself upon a girl. Then she wept, and hoped the Coes shot his head off, so he found out what it was like to get hurt.

She went on in that way, while he sat at the office table checking the action of Reed Coe's .44. It was a prime revolver, and had been worked by a smith to a fine and easy response. The trigger-press was lighter than Link liked, would take a fine hand if you were shooting fast, to place your shots.

If he needed the weapon though, needed the extra five rounds, he'd be glad enough to take care with the lighter trigger-press. Must be nervous, at that, to figure he might need extra ammunition in a fight. Had been his experience that few fights with guns lasted more than four or five rounds, each side. So he was likely a little nervous.

The coaching-girl had quieted down. Though still talking, she was at least not yelling and cursing as she had been. Might be that Coe had been right about the Turks and their bowstrings . . .

"We could be famous," she said. "And we could run this town, lock, stock, and barrel. We'd be more famous than Wild Bill and Calamity Jane!" She was standing at the little window in the cell door, peering out at him. Link could see the tip of her nose as she talked.

Damn that Buntline!

Not that she was so far wrong, especially about running Colt Creek. If the Coes were broken . . . *If*, there'd be money waiting for the man who took their place. If he wanted to take their place . .

Something for a dead-broke drifter who'd damn sure seen better days, and was unlikely to see better days ahead—something for that fellow to think about.

A little more than an hour later, full dark, someone came to the office door and knocked softly on it. Could be no citizen inquiring about the girl's screams and cursing, because she'd been quiet for some time. Odd about that, strange how people are made. He'd been annoyed enough at the notion that she'd come making up love to him, yet he was . . . his feelings were hurt, after all, when he found her interested in no such thing. Wanting to be famous, like Jane and Hickok. Good God!

He got up from the table at the knock, tucked the .44 into his waistband, went to the door, and stood for a moment, listening, standing to one side of the panelling in case someone fired through. It seemed early for it, but Busey may have lost his patience, forced the pace.

"Who is it?"

Link didn't understand the answer, at first. Couldn't tell what the man was saying. Then the fellow spoke again. It was a colored man—George, from the Rose. Keeping clear, Link reached down to unlock the door.

"Come in."

The colored man walked hesitantly through the door, and no one came in after him.

"What is it, George?" Link swung the door shut, and locked it.

George looked sick, older than he had, and trembling. "Oh, Mister," he said, "they're killin' Mister MacDuff. They ast him about you, all kin' of things. Then they took him on out back an' they killin' him!" He had his hands pressed along his trouser legs to stop them shaking, but his arms were trembling anyway.

"They tell you to come get me?"

"Nossir . . . nossir. Was my idea to come git you. Most everybody run on out of the Rose when they come in. Some mean folks stay to see the fun, but most everybody run out. They don't want to be around them men, an' I don' blame 'em!"

Link put his hand on the man's shoulder. "Now, you

216

rest easy; I'll do what I can." Billy Coe, or Busey, more likely, had picked MacDuff to be the one to draw him to them. It was clever. Another man, he might have left in their hands, and let them do their worst, rather than come running to them where they waited.

Another man. Not MacDuff. He remembered the saloon owner weeping over the murder of his friend, the freighter who ran all the way to Philadelphia. Besides, he owed MacDuff too damn much from the cash drawer.

"All right," he said, to no one in particular. "All right."

"For God's sake," the girl shouted from the cell, "let me out to help you! We can handle those sneaks!"

"Now, listen," Link said to the colored man, "you stay here. Don't come back to the Rose till it's all well over." George seemed more than willing to do that, and kept nodding yes, he would. "Another thing. That girl in there?" (She waws still shouting through the cell door.) George nodded yes. "I don't want her out of that cell on any excuse whatever, do you understand that?" Nod. "You can stay here if you want, but if I come back and find you've let her out of there, I'll have your hide—you understand that?"

George's last nod wasn't enough. Link looked at him until he added a "Yessir."

"All right, lock this door when I go out—and keep it locked."

"Yessir."

Link checked to see he had Coe's .44 in his belt, stooped slightly to touch the handle of the toothpick in his right boot-top, and, straightening, touched the butt of the Bisley lightly with his fingers, something he didn't usually do.

Must be feeling shy . . .

217

He unlocked the door, opened it, and walked out. As the swamper closed the door behind him, Link heard the girl call, "You're a damn fool, Fred Link!"

Well, he likely was.

He stepped out of the office, and into an empty town. The streets lay vacant, buildings shuttered, silent, no lights showing in the gathering dark. A dog wandered under the boardwalk down the block. Nothing else living showed.

The shooting of Reed Coe had tripped the town's nerve; the people didn't want to see the rest of it.

Link began walking down Main toward the Rose. Halfway down the first block he passed a little barrelken named Curley's. The small hole-in-the-wall, always noisy with fights and drunken singing, was quiet as a grave.

Link walked on by.

A restaurant without a name was on the right. He'd never cared to try and eat there, though drovers seemed to favor it—probably served heavy on the canned tomatoes, fried out in pork drippings. That, and peach mash. Fair enough food, for wornout cow pokers, but the smell had always put Link off. Might not have, if he hadn't already fed in the Chinaman's kitchen.

Nobody in that restaurant tonight. Range bosses likely kept their men out of town. Somewhere, back deep in the basement, there would be gluey kettle of peach mash bubbling away with no cowboys to stop it up with stone-hard biscuits at thirty cents a serving. The damn fool things those people would spend their money on. Shouldn't complain, though, made enough money off them, with girls and gambling. Unfair advantage, really, considering how hard drovers' lives

218

were. They generally came into a town desperate for pleasure, and most any pleasure would do.

Easy to make a living off people like that.

He saw the Rose's big hanging sign up ahead. Poorly painted thing—looked as much like a big white cow on that sign as a white rose . . .

Link felt short of breath, and stopped at a corner, just where the boardwalk steps went down. He put out a hand and leaned against a building wall. He felt a little sick to his stomach, and out of breath, too. Knew what it was—it sure as hell was nothing he had eaten. Those boys had him scared to death—or something did.

The arm he was bracing himself with was trembling, and he felt cold sweat on him. Scared to death.

It was because of the way he'd done Reed Coe. That was a bad one, shooting that chap to pieces that way. Never had a chance in this world. It was more like a hanging, than a fight. Murder, was what it was.

Brought death closer, some way, killing Coe like that. Made it plainer, closer. And Reed had still tried, having no chance at all. Had known, at the end, that it was more than a drifting bartender sitting in the next chair to him. Had known who Link was, without ever knowing his real name. Death, with a pistol on his knee. Death in a striped sheet.

Link straightened up, and wiped his face on the fringed buckskin sleeve of his jacket. It wasn't Billy Coe and Busey who'd made him sink and sweat, then. It had only been another man's ghost. Link took a deep breath of the cool evening air. No doubt a few pairs of eyes were watching, figuring the deputy had gone shakey on a fight. It was true enough. He'd been afraid before, under half a dozen names, and he'd taken his deep breaths and got on with it.

Besides, no matter how sickly scared he ever got, the Bisley Colt's was never frightened. Nor the long knife in his boot.

CHAPTER 16

LINK WENT through a board fence into the back yard of the Rose. Through the trees along the western side of the field bordering the outskirts of town, a pale yellow rising moon shone broken by branches.

Long, faint moon shadows streaked the cluttered yard, the lumber stacks, well pump, and outhouse. Coal oil lamps blazed from the Rose's kitchen, and Link heard a piano tinkling from the bar room. It was a quiet night, with no wind blowing. Only flickering bats, outlined for an instant against bright windows, then gone.

Link stood for a few moments, watching and listening. Then he saw someone sitting on the kitchen steps. He thought for a moment it was MacDuff, then he saw the moonlight frosted on a silver-grey beard, tied up with string.

He walked through the yard toward the kitchen, and the Chinaman came to meet him.

"Mister Leslie," the old man said, "you have come —but, for something, you have come too late."

"Where's MacDuff?"

"Where we will all be." The old man walked out

221

into the yard, beckoning Link to follow him. He walked to the outhouse.

When Link came up to him, the old man opened the rough plank door.

At first, Link saw nothing there in the darkness. He stepped closer, starting to call MacDuff's name—and then saw clearly MacDuff's legs and feet, his shabby brogues and clumsy corduroy spats, sticking up out of the shit hole. He'd been stuffed in head first, to drown.

Link shoved the old man aside, jumped into the cramped little shack, seized MacDuff's legs, and with a back-wrenching effort, jerked the man loose in that close pit and, bending his knees, heaving, heaving with all his strength, began to draw the man up and out.

When MacDuff was free of it, Link dragged the body outside, dragged it down to the pump, and working the handle desperately, pumped water in a stream over MacDuff's shit-caked head and chest. Then he bent over him, as the old Chinaman watched, and wrenched MacDuff's mouth open, clawed the manure out of it, rinsed the gaping face clean, the white dead eyes, rolled back in his death agony, white throat and forehead. All washed clean.

Link looked down at the corpse, then stooped and closed MacDuff's eyes. He motioned to the Chinaman to work the pump, and he washed his hands clean under the surging water, then dried them on his neckerchief.

"Go get the undertaker," he said to the old man. "Tell him there's work for him. And more coming."

Then he went up the kitchen stairs, and into the White Rose.

He walked through the empty kitchen, down the long hallway, and out beside the bar, in the big front room. All the lamps were lit, and a man Link knew named Dixon was playing the old upright piano that stood against the opposite wall. He was playing "Marching Through Georgia," playing it at a very fast tempo.

Twenty or thirty men around the room were sitting at tables drinking beer, and watching a rosy-faced man in a plaid suit dancing with one of the fat sisters.

The fellow was very big, and bulky—fat-looking in the face, ruddy and chubby-cheeked. He had muddy brown eyes, shaved his face, and wore dark blond hair in little spit curls across his forehead. He was dressed to the nines in a fine-cut Chicago suit of yellow plaid, and wore patent leather high-button shoes on his heat, prancing feet.

He was a wonderful dancer, much better than the girl, and leaped and spun and tossed his head, flung his shining shoes out pointed as he high-kicked and cake-walked to the beat. He sidled this way, and sidled back, and shook his big butt as he danced, gesturing like an actor with his hands. When he spun and turned and whirled around, the handle of a pearl-grip pistol shone poking from his trouser pocket.

The cuffs of his fine yellow plaid jacket were dark with water-damp from the pump outside, and peeping from his left cuff as he snapped his fingers, doing a little jump step backwards and forwards was the small quick glitter of a finger hook. He had a large straight razor up his sleeve.

While dancing at his best, spinning 'round the clumsy girl like a fairground ride, Henry Busey had still marked Link at once, and the big man, kicking high, looked back to the bar, and gestured with a graceful hand to where Link stood, just beyond the end of the bar.

Link turned his head, and met Coe's glance.

As the big man had been bright, and moving, and shining in the light, so Billy Coe was dark as any shadow. He did not look like a man others called "Billy." He was shorter than Reed had been, but wore the same long face. But his face was still as stone, and white as polished stone as well. His eyes were black, and MacDuff's dead eyes, all white, had been no deader.

He wore a fine grey banker's suit, black boots, and tied down to his right leg, Texas style, a Remington .44 in a worn brown holster.

He looked as dangerous as a falling wall.

It occurred to Link, in that moment, that these two men, after all, might be able to kill him. Not and walk away themselves, of course. But kill him, all the same.

The roughs in the Rose that night—the town and country louts tough enough, or stupid enough to want to see a very fierce fight—now had fallen silent. Only Dixon kept playing the piano, probably afraid of Busey if he stopped.

Billy Coe spoke.

"What's your name?" he said to Link, meaning Link's real name. He had a very deep voice.

"If you knew, you'd piss your pants," Link said. And Dixon stopped playing, and Billy Coe drew his gun.

Coe had the kind of draw that Link had seen only once before, on an old Border Ruffian. It was simple and very fast. Coe pulled the pistol straight up out of the holster, cocked his wrist, and fired. It took a strong wrist; and it was all done in less than a quarter second, timed by any stop-watch.

Link drew and shot Coe through the belly just as Coe's Remington went off, and something, Coe's

224

bullet, snatched at Link's left arm and tugged him a little around.

Where was Busey?

But he couldn't leave off Coe now, or the fellow would kill him. Coe, standing straight against the bar, his long face unmoved, untroubled, fired a second time and missed as Link fell sideways to the floor and shot Coe again, falling.

Coe fired again after Link hit rolling, and Link felt his right foot struck a hard blow. His ankle felt broken from it. He shot at Coe again—and missed. Link heard furniture smashing, and looked across the room to see Henry Busey, grinning, charging down on him, tables and chairs spinning out of his way. The small nickel-plated revolver twinkled in his hand.

Link shot at Busey from the floor, and missed him clean as the big man hit the floor with a crash, ducking. A bullet snapped just past Link's face; the wind of it stung his left eye, and he turned and saw Billy Coe kneeling by the bar holding his revolver in a two-handed grip, sighting through the smoke. Link shot him through the head, and the back of his head flew off and his brains spattered down the front of the bar, wet grey and red against the dark mahogany.

A bullet came stinging, and hit Link like a hammer just above his hip. He thought, "Christ, that's killed me!" but was able to scramble up on one knee as Busey was up again, lunging through overturned chairs, firing.

Link's ears were ringing from the explosions. He saw the big man suddenly swing around to shoot down at a fellow lying on the floor, some frightened fellow trying to stay safe. Busey fired down into the man's back, turned to look for Link again, saw him and came shooting. Link dropped the Bisley and tried to reach to his waistband for Reed Coe's Peacemaker, but his left arm wouldn't go.

He rolled onto the floor again, trying to get in behind a pot-belly stove before Busey killed him.

He could hear Busey laughing, saw him ducking past a table to get around the stove. Link reached with his right hand, got hold of the Peacemaker, pulled it, and fired as Busey came clear.

He hit the man, heard the thump of the bullet going into him; then Link scrambled and got up on his good foot and stood to face Busey across the stove. They fired together and Busey's bullet struck the Peacemaker and knocked it back into Link's face. It was a heavy blow and it blinded him.

Link fell back, but hit a table and was able to hold onto it. He felt blood running down his face, and stooped to reach into his boot for the toothpick. He got the knife out, wiped blood from his eyes with his sleeve, and saw Busey getting up from his hands and knees beside the stove. Link's bullet had blown his lower jaw away.

Busey heaved himself up, his eyes blinking, spouting blood from the splintered ruin of his jaw, raised the shiny little pistol, pointed it at Link and pulled the trigger. It clicked empty, and the big man, his bright suit ruined with blood, shook his sleeve to palm his razor, flicked it open, and came for Link to kill him with it. He swung full-armed at Link, slipped in his own blood and struck the stove chimney.

Link lunged into him, grappled the big man in spattering blood, and drove the blade of the toothpick into his belly.

Busey stiffened, his belly muscles seizing up the double-edged blade so that Link could barely twist it. Link set himself, blind again from the blood in his eyes, and wrenched upward on the knife handle with all his strength. He felt the razor blad against the back of his left shoulder. The edge felt cold as ice as Busey drew it down.

Suddenly the toothpick moved and the long blade jolted and ran free up through the big man's belly. The blade sliced up, and Henry Busey's bowels came out of him.

CHAPTER 17

HIGH ON the ridge, where the wind, hot with afternoon sun, came combing through the tall grass, Link sat the hammer-headed brown, looking down at his town.

Below, Colt Creek lay almost quiet. The church bell was ringing for three o'clock service. There would be a church supper after that to which he was invited, as town marshal.

The young doctor with the blond beard had been glad enough to treat Link again. "You are an oddity, indeed," he'd said, examining Link's wounds, reviewing the scars that striped his body. "Have you read the novel, 'Frankenstein,' Marshal? Well, you are coming, more and more, to resemble my unfortunate colleague's fictional creation."

"I didn't read it."

"You should," the young doctor had said. "There's a moral there that might equally apply to that too-ready revolver of yours." With that, he'd untied one of the bandages the Chinaman had done, threaded his needle, and began to sew.

Could have been worse. A cut forehead. A two-bit sized chunk shot out of the flesh and muscle of Link's upper left arm. A long, clean razor cut along his left shoulder blade. A bullet in his right hip bone, but barely stuck in the surface; it had been slowed by his gunbelt. And a sprained right ankle, due to his boot heel being shot away.

Link had had worse than any of it. The wound Stern had given him had been worse. Still, these had kept him on his back on a narrow cell cot for more than a week, with only the old Chinaman and Charmian Swazee for nurses.

Nancy Plum had not come near him. Sore about missing her chance for Wild West Glory, he supposed.

He had got some reading done. Dickens' "Great Expectation," and "Frankenstein." The young doctor had been right; there was an apt moral there. Link enjoyed the Dickens more.

The sorest trial of that bedtime had been old Charmian's tries at out-cooking the Chinaman. A lot of ragout dinners had had to be slipped into the slop bucket. Link figured that Charmian's cooking had set him back two days, at least.

Then, when he was up and walking, some other people came around. The banker, Nordstrom. Postal Service fellow. Perry Patterson, from the livery. And Mister Forster, the hide merchant. They all had this or that to say, and what it all amounted to was, "How about running our town for us?" Or, at least, "How about seeing to it that no one else runs our town?"

Link was still thinking that over, when Wilse Coe came to call.

Smiling, handsome, beautifully dressed in New York City clothes, the Yale man seemed mighty pleased to shake Link's hand. Then they sat in rockers on Mister Forster's front porch; Link had just finished his supper there. Mrs. Forster's pork chops had been breaded in a batter handed down from her grand-mother, who had cooked that very dish for Alexander Hamilton, in Trenton, New Jersey.

"Heavens," Wilse Coe had said, smiling, "I feel lucky to be alive! You've certainly made mincemeat of the Coe family!" It didn't seem to trouble him.

"I would have killed you too if you'd been in the Rose that night."

"I don't doubt it for a minute, Marshal." He made a rueful face that reminded Link of Reed. "And I suppose we deserved such a judgement; we'd been very bad." He winked.

Link reflected that there wasn't much use in killing lawyers, anyway. Others, often even worse, would spring up to take their place. Wilse had cheerfully gone to offer his services—the services of Rocking-D, as well—in regularizing Colt Creek's administration. He could practically guarantee that Boise would let a reasonable arrangement ride.

"What does your Daddy think of that?" Link said.

"Father . . . well, Father hasn't been in good health lately. He's quite old, you know."

Older now, for certain sure. But perhaps not past it, either.

They'd left it at that. A possible gentleman's agreement. Wilse had risen, gone to the door to thank Mrs. Forster for the shady hospitality of her front porch— to accuse her, jokingly, of serving her famous pork chops without inviting him—had then shaken hands again with Link, winked at him, sauntered out to his buggy, and driven off. Likely to be, Link thought, in time the most dangerous Coe of all.

There had been more of that sort of thing—business offers of one kind or another. A partnership in a parlor house; a loading fee over at the stockyard—just to be around, if the men made trouble.

Link listened to all of them.

He talked to Patterson about the mute girl at the stable, Patterson's niece, it turned out, and had the doctor examine her.

The doctor's wife, big boned, sweet-faced Quaker girl from St. Louis, had offered to care for the girl. And when Link had told her and her doctor husband both that the girl would likely be better off in a well run brothel, the sweet-faced wife had turned mighty tough on him, held the mute girl in an iron grip, and run Link right out of her house.

It gave him a better opinion of the mouthy young doctor, to have caught him a wife with such backbone to her.

That had been his good turn. He didn't think he'd done any other. The fierce men he had killed—men like himself in all important wawys—would return to Colt Creek, only with different faces, different manners to their doings.

Now the town was his. To hold it, he need not even kill another man. For anything of that sort, he had only to hire two or three hard young boys from Texas, or the Territory, to be his deputies. They would gladly do his killings for him.

The town was his. And, in good time, he would win the Plum girl back to bed. So, in ease, his drifting days would be done. What any man could ask for, he would have.

Link sat the brown a little while longer, looking down the long, rolling slope to where Colt Creek bent around the town. The church bell still rang. He could make out each house, could see the wagons in the streets.

It was a fine, hot, sunny day in Spring; the wind from the mountains cooled his face. Link looked down once more, then turned his horse's head, and rode away.

BORDER RIDERS

ROBERT STEELMAN

Lieutenant David Pine rode into his hometown after six years' absence to find that things had changed. A shadow of fear hung over the town—fear of the ruthless killer, General Pancho Villa.

When Villa's hell-bent gang stormed in, Pine witnessed a slaughter that sent him thundering across the border after the murderers, and into the hands of the desperado Paco Mora. To save his life, David Pine, U.S. Army, was forced to fight side by side with the most vicious outlaws in history!

Before it was over, Pine would be branded a criminal. He'd spill blood on both sides of the border, as he rode a cruel trail that could lead either to freedom—or a noose!

WESTERN

0-8439- 2059-9

$2.25

THE OTHER SIDE OF THE CANYON

ROMER ZANE GREY

THE OTHER SIDE OF THE CANYON marks the return to print of one of Zane Grey's strongest characters, Laramie Nelson, first introduced in Grey's novel RAIDERS OF SPANISH PEAKS. Laramie was a seasoned Indian fighter, an incomparable tracker, and one of the deadliest gunhands the West had ever known.

In these stories, Romer Zane Grey, son of the master storyteller, continues Laramie's adventures as he takes on a gang of train robbers, a gold thief, and a sharpshooting woman wanted for murder!

WESTERN
0-8439
2041-6
$2.75

GUN TROUBLE
IN TONTO BASIN

ROMER ZANE GREY

Gun Trouble In Tonto Basin signals the reappearance of Arizona Ames, the title character of one of Zane Grey's most memorable novels. Young Rich Ames came to lead the life of a range drifter after he participated in a gunfight that left two men dead. Ames' skill earned him a reputation as one of the fastest guns in the West.

In these splendid stories, Arizona Ames comes home to find his range and his family haunted by the shadow of a terror they dare not name!

WESTERN
0-8439-2098-X
$2.75

THE RIDER OF DISTANT TRAILS

ROMER ZANE GREY

The Rider Of Distant Trails marks the return to print of one of Zane Grey's most memorable characters, Buck Duane, first introduced in Grey's novel *Lone Star Ranger*. Forced to turn outlaw as a young man, Buck later teamed up with Captain Jim MacNelly of the Texas Rangers and proved himself to be the Ranger's deadliest gun.

In these stories, Romer Zane Grey, son of the master storyteller, continues Buck's adventures in Texas and as he takes on outlaws who are terrorizing ranches and towns in this tough cattle country!

WESTERN
0-8439-2082-3
$2.75